THE FATE OF THE
LADY EMMA

THE FATE OF THE LADY EMMA

Paul Lund and Harry Ludlam

NEW ENGLISH LIBRARY/TIMES MIRROR

First published in Great Britain in
1978 by New English Library

© 1978 by Paul Lund and Harry Ludlam

First NEL paperback edition April 1979

NEL Books are published by
New English Library Limited from
Barnard's Inn, Holborn,
London EC1N 2JR
Made and printed in Great Britain by
Hunt Barnard Printing Ltd.,
Aylesbury, Bucks

45004101 8

1

In one of the cheerless tin-roofed huts that formed the Naval base at Kirkwall, in the Orkneys, the tedious day began as usual. As it had yesterday, and would again tomorrow.

This hut was the Regulating Office. A kind of Labour Exchange, with the same dead, defeating air of the real thing. Behind a counter that important personage the Regulating Petty Officer, and his small staff, dealt with a never-ending stream of paperwork. Facing the counter were wooden benches on which sat a number of dispirited ratings, smoking, talking, reading. Waiting for some notice to be taken of them, some word of their future to trickle down from the Lords of the Admiralty.

Each morning they came, the new sailors, the 'sprogs'. Some were found ships immediately, others were told, 'Yours isn't in yet – report back here at 1400.' The disappointed ones would trail back at that hour, only to be told to report again the following morning. And so the cycle went on, with the brand new sailors kicking their heels and idling away their days, staring out into the harbour and watching the trawlers bobbing at their mooring buoys, trying to picture what life would be like on board them.

But for one rating at least, this late morning, the wearisome routine was ended.

'Ordinary-Seaman Price!' barked the bull-necked R.P.O.

He got up from his bench, one of the quieter ones, with a less savage haircut than some and the assurance that came of being a year or two older than most of the rank and file. Intelligent looking, too. We have a right one here, thought the R.P.O.

'Report to the *Lady Emma* forthwith. Off to your billet, pick up your gear, proceed to the harbour and catch the first drifter out – all right? Look lively, sailor!'

The R.P.O. turned back to his paperwork, growling irritably to himself. 'What did I do to deserve this bloody job? I should be back in Pompey . . .'

Price left the hut and collected his belongings from the Scout hall. There, for five nights, he had slept in his overcoat on a mattress on the hard floor with wind, snow and sleet driving in through the broken window panes; sleeping with his arms round his kitbag to foil the nightly raiders who broke open padlocks or cut out the bottoms of kitbags to replenish the gear they had lost or flogged.

Good riddance! With kitbag on shoulder and small suitcase in hand, he made his way down to the harbour. On the jetty he joined a small group of other sprogs destined for different vessels. It was a grey January day with flurries of snow and a keen wind which whipped up the waters of Kirkwall Bay into a pattern of white horses. Other sailors busy around the harbour were muffled in thick jerseys, work-coats and balaclavas, which made the new men even more conscious that they stood out a mile, and cold with it, in their new regulation issue Naval over-coats and caps whose unsullied ribbons read 'H.M. Patrol Service'. As the wind lashed their faces and tugged at their clothing they stamped their feet and shivered, exchanging few words except to curse the weather, the war, or the Navy itself.

They saw the old liberty drifter making calls at several trawlers; it seemed to take an interminable time. Then here she was, with the sound of lusty singing coming from her deck. She came bucking and rolling up to the jetty and a batch of liberty-men, in their Number Ones and polished boots and tiddley bows, came swinging ashore. As the drifter emptied, Price and his companions climbed on board and were off to start at last their life at sea.

As they steamed across the bay Price recalled the final chal-lenging send-off to his squad by an instructor at Lowestoft, headquarters of the Royal Naval Patrol Service.

'You bloody awful lot! You're going to sea in old fishing trawlers and drifters fitted up with guns. *If* you're lucky you might get one of them bloody big Asdic trawlers that go out hunting U-boats – *if* you're lucky!'

So they were lucky.

'These are the pick of the Patrol Service fleet?' said a little

Scot from Glasgow incredulously, echoing his thoughts. 'Don't look up to much, do they?'

As they approached one of the trawlers Price ran his eyes over her weatherbeaten exterior with its drab coat of black-and-tan paint and the daubs of red lead on her sides. The four-inch gun mounted for'ard looked incongruous on a vessel plainly built for peacefully fishing the seas, but the curve of her lines, from the rounded stern to the rising sheer of her high bow, had a certain grace about it. As they passed the stern her name came into view. LADY EMMA.

'Good luck, mate,' said the little Scot nervously when they came alongside, level with the trawler's deck. Price stepped on board with his gear and the drifter pulled away.

The trawler's Quartermaster, wrapped in an overcoat and apparent gloom, looked him up and down with tired eyes.

'The new hand? You've missed dinner. Messdeck's that way.' He pointed, lost interest and wandered off.

As he hoisted up his kit again Price was aware of an officer and a bulky, bearded seaman having a brisk and somewhat spiky conversation close by. The bearded one put in the parting shot.

' . . . And I'm the bugger who does all the work on board this bloody old tub!' he complained loudly as he walked away.

The officer saw Price.

'I'll speak to you later, Michael,' he called limply after the retreating figure. Then, 'Who are you?'

Price saluted and told him.

'Very good. Join the messdeck.'

The officer frowned, turned on his heel and made off resolutely in the direction of the departed seaman.

Price lugged his kit across to the messdeck hatch and lifted aside the canvas flap.

'Drop it down, mate,' called a voice, and he let go the kitbag and followed it down the ladder.

'Welcome to the *Lady Emma* – what a ship!'

' 'Ardship, you mean.'

'*Altmark*'s about it.'

'Rolling old bastard.'

'No leave, no pay, no sweet Fanny Adams . . .'

'Are you a good sailor? She bumps a bit.'

Price looked around at the blur of faces on the messdeck.

'Your first ship?'

He nodded.

'Gawd 'elp you, then.'

A figure wearing a disreputable leather watch-coat, tattered and stiff from salt water, came down the ladder with a rush, singing at the top of his voice.

'*Jee*-pers . . . *cree*-pers, where d'yer get those *pee*-pers . . .'

He stopped on seeing Price.

'Are you the new hand? Welcome to His Majesty's Trawler *Lady Emma*, the pride of the British Navy! The terror of the seas, the scourge of the U-boats. How the German Fleet tremble when they hear that the old *Emma* is at sea again! Bring all guns to bear on the enemy – and the spud-thrower. Don't shoot till you see the whites of their eyes . . .'

'Aw, get stuffed, James,' shouted someone.

'Don't mind me,' continued the man called James. 'I'm quite mad. We're all mad.'

He spoke in an educated, public school kind of voice, although his lively face with its square chin sported several days' scrubby growth of beard. He grinned, and his hazel-green eyes offered friendship.

'You'll be mad, too, when you've been on this job six months. What's your name?'

'Price. Where do I put all this gear?'

James looked at him keenly for a few seconds.

'I'll show you. Let's see, whose bunk can you have? Ah, here you are, my friend. A sound, well-furnished bed on the ground floor, all mod cons. The last tenant was an earnest student of navigation, pilotage and so forth, but became a little eccentric later on. One day he refused to obey an order – told Jimmy the One to do something most extraordinary with the wheel . . .'

'Stick it up his arse,' said a willing interpreter.

' . . . and departed from our midst, never to return.'

'The bloke before him was screwy too,' chimed in another voice.

'So he was!' said James. 'Funny, but they all seem to go bonkers in this bunk. Never mind, chum, perhaps you'll have better luck.'

He waved an arm.

'Above you dwells our regal Bunts. He sleeps most of the time and will step on your face and clout you with his bunk-board as he climbs in, but don't let that worry you.'

'At least I don't go reciting bloody poetry to my next-below, like you,' retorted the signalman, looking up from the letter he was writing.

8

'No soul, our Bunts,' went on James, unabashed. 'Here are your two drawers under the bunk. Fill them up with what you want and stow the rest of your kit in a locker. You can draw your watch-coat, seaboots and oilskins from our good cox'n later.'

Price deposited his gear and looked round the messdeck, which in peacetime had been the *Lady Emma*'s fish hold when she had gone deep-sea trawling up to remote Bear Island and the icy Barents Sea. There were bunks all round the walls – called 'bulkheads' from now on, he remembered. There were four tables, and a blazing coal fire in the centre of the big room, surrounded by wooden forms on which were gathered most of the messdeck's occupants.

James followed his gaze. 'Luxurious, isn't it, lad? You don't find many trawler crews with a real coal fire – they have to put up with Nissen hut stoves.'

He was still shrewdly sizing up the newcomer.

'How are your sealegs?'

'I haven't tried them out yet.'

'Well, that's honest. What brought you to this old bucket? You look cut out for a cruiser.'

'I didn't want the big ships.'

'You may live to regret it, dear boy.'

Price shrugged.

'Leave him alone, James. He doesn't need your bloody advice.'

'No charge,' said James. 'See you later, kid.' He crossed to his own bunk.

Price flushed. He was twenty-two years old and the high-handed James looked to be scarcely three or four years older. He was not used to being called 'kid'. Later, he was unpacking his kit when a voice from above yelled, 'Tea-oh!' Everyone suddenly came alive and scrambled for the ladder down to the eating mess in the after part of the ship, jostling each other as they went. He followed as eagerly as the rest, for he was hungry. To his surprise the table was well laden with bread and butter, scones, cakes and trifles. Everyone fell to with relish.

'You seem to do well for eats,' he said to those seated around him.

There was a roar of laughter.

'Don't fool yourself,' said a big, raw-boned seaman. 'This is our long-delayed Christmas tea.'

'Delayed for weeks,' moaned the man beside him, belligerently pushing more cake into his mouth. 'And a happy 1942 to us all.'

'And let somebody blow up Hitler so that they can send us all home to our lovin' wives.'

'Fat bloody chance . . . '

Later, Price reported to the Coxswain, a dour Scots Petty Officer with an abrasive voice. He noted down the details of the new arrival.

'You'll be a dayman till you find your legs, which means you'll get all-night-in. You don't get that very often, so make the most of it while you can.'

Price went back to the messdeck, where most men sat yarning on the benches in front of the fire. He began to write a letter.

'Are you a C.W.?'

He looked up, startled, to find James perched on a corner of the table, watching him.

'C.W.?' he answered, as though mystified.

'Yes, commission candidate.'

Price prayed that his face would not redden and give him away, for he knew full well what a C.W. man was. He was one. But he had been strongly warned that the C.W., or White Paper Candidate, was the lowest form of life known to the lower deck – that loathsome specimen of sailorhood, the officer-to-be. 'C.W. candidates, we shit 'em!' was the cry. The crew suspected them of being in league with the Wardroom, while the officers, remembering how they themselves had been roughly treated, saw no reason why their successors shouldn't suffer just as much as they. In a big ship there might be some thirty C.W.s together – safety in numbers – but in a trawler, Price had been warned, a C.W. man could find himself alone – 'And they'll bloody well kick you to death if they find out!'

James was grinning, almost as though he guessed the thoughts racing through the new man's mind.

'Oh well, don't worry if you're not a C.W. You soon will be. What's your first name?'

'Peter.'

'All right, Peter Price. Supper's up soon.'

After the meal, Price had returned to his bunk to finish stowing his belongings when there was the sound of hearty singing and clatter upon clatter on the upper deck. The libertymen had returned. They came noisily down to the messdeck and went talkatively to the fire or their bunks, all except one quiet boy of barely eighteen who was quick to notice that Price's bunk was now occupied. He looked at Price from a distance, then approached him.

'Welcome on board,' he said, holding out his hand. 'My name's Eric Brewster.'

Price felt that he had seldom appreciated a handshake more than at that moment.

'Is this your first patrol?' said Brewster.

'Yes.'

'It's my second. You'll be all right. Have a Woodbine?'

'Thanks.' Price did not want the cigarette but he took it. They talked some more before the boy went over to his own bunk, and Brewster was quick to elicit in a roundabout way that Price did not have a regular girl.

'I have. Her name's Enid. Enid Stapleton. We're going steady – I'll show you her picture.' He dug into his pocket and produced a snapshot from a wallet. She was small and cuddlesome, shyly smiling as she stood close to an empty clothes line in the back garden.

'It's not a good one, but when I get leave we're going to a studio to have one taken together.'

'She's very pretty,' said Price.

'Yes,' said Brewster proudly, then, 'I expect you've known lots of girls.'

'Some.'

'Enid and me live in the same street. The *Emma* isn't a bad ship, you know.'

'No?'

'There's a lot worse. If there's anything you want to know . . .'

'Thanks.'

Price drifted off to sleep that night going over the parting lecture by a tough Petty Officer before his party of sprogs had left Lowestoft for the long journey up to the Orkneys.

'You do two weeks out on patrol, all on your lonesome, and four days in harbour, one or two days of which are spent coaling ship – about the hardest job you'll get, and the dirtiest. You get liberty runs ashore to Kirkwall each time you are in, and every six or seven months you go down to Aberdeen or Grimsby for a refit and boiler-clean, which gives you a few weeks' leave. The Northern Patrol extends from the Orkneys as far north as Iceland. You challenge every ship, and you're after U-boats or Jerry surface raiders trying to sneak out into the Atlantic to get at our convoys . . .'

11

Or, as one grizzled patrol veteran had summed it up for him more graphically before departing happily from Lowestoft for duties in the South of England, 'Oh, it's a *bastard* of a life, mate. A reet *bastard*!'

2

Next morning, as young Brewster was detailed off for storeboat duties, Price somewhat warily accepted James's grandiose invitation to show him around the ship.

'This is the P.O.'s mess – take your cap off when you enter, they're rather touchy.' It was a small, comfortable room with curtained bunks of polished oak on each bulkhead. 'If you get to be messman here you're all right – a thousand times better than fetching and carrying for our lot.

'Here's the galley. Keep out unless you're messman – the cook's notoriously temperamental. One wrong word and he goes for his chopper . . .

'That's the engine-room, down below. Keep out of that, too – the Chief's temperamental as well. He's an elderly chap, in his fifties, fighting his second war against the Germans. He's suspicious of everything that breathes, and guards his stokers like a mother hen, when he isn't giving 'em hell . . .

'Here's the twin point-five, worked by three men – did they tell you about these guns?'

They were now on the port side, aft.

'And this peculiar contrivance,' said James, affectionately patting a long, almost vertical piece of piping with hose-tubing connected to the base, 'is the Holman projector. It works by steam. You drop a Mills bomb down the spout, press the foot pedal to release the steam, and up goes the jolly old bomb and brings down Jerry planes by the dozen. At least, that's the theory. In reality it's a frightening thing and totally unreliable – s best use is for firing spuds at other trawlers as we pass.'

They continued walking.

'These are the depth-charge rails, and here are more D.C.s in their throwers. You'll bang your face on them getting along the deck in the dark – everyone does at first.'

They turned and neared the hatch to the officers' quarters. The *Lady Emma* carried four officers, including the captain.

'This is the Wardroom – the holy-of-holies. Cap off, don't forget, when you go down there. It's the place where our esteemed officers drink their gin.'

At this point the Wardroom door opened and the officer Price had encountered on boarding the trawler emerged. Ignoring Price he snapped at his companion: 'Have you seen Michael?'

'No, sir,' said James with instant innocence.

The officer grimly compressed his lips and stalked off in a smouldering rage.

'That's Mr Sibley, our No. 2,' explained James. 'Better known as "Cross-Buckets".

'Now for our main armament. There it is, the four-inch – you could be elected one of its crew. "Guns" loves it like a baby – always changing its nappies . . .

'There's the washplace. Very uncomfortable at sea, being right up in the bows. You don't wash when it's rough, or even think about it. And the Heads – lavatories, you know. They can be dicey, too – you have to choose the best times to go. Sometimes it's a long wait. If it's only a slash you want you needn't bother, just help yourself anywhere – only beware the No. 1's warning stuck on the notice board.' He grinned. 'Now, I've got to see Sparks in the wireless cabin – can you find your way back?'

'Yes, thanks.'

Left to his own resources, Price wandered until he found the notice board, and there read the No. 1's warning.

'It has come to my notice that certain members of this crew are using the deck of one of H.M. ships as a urinal. This is a disgusting practice which will cease forthwith (signed) First Lieutenant.'

He had returned to the deck and was staring over the ship's side, looking at the coldly lapping waters of Kirkwall Bay, when the officer known as 'Cross-Buckets' suddenly reappeared. He was around thirty years old, with a sour face, puggish nose, and something evidently niggling on his mind. He stopped in his tracks.

'Ah, you, now let me see, you're –'

'Price, sir.'

'Price – the new man, are you?'

'Yes, sir, just joined ship.'

'Of course, yes, new man. Do you know Michael, the Asdic rating?'

'No, sir.'

'Hmmm.' The officer's mind then seemed to clear. 'You are not in the rig of the day,' he snapped.

'Rig of the day, sir?'

'Yes, overalls – *rig of the day*!'

The officer walked off. Price went below and changed into his overalls.

'That's right, lad,' said William Campbell approvingly, as he presented himself in his working clothes. Campbell was the 'Buffer' who handed out the duties on behalf of the Coxswain. 'Ye have a turn as Quartermaster – come and see me later.'

In the afternoon the libertymen had long gone ashore when, at the appointed time, Price was taken up to the bridge by Campbell and his duties explained. His main task seemed to be to watch the signal station of the Naval base ashore and alert the *Emma*'s signalman if they called up the ship.

'D'ye know the morse?' asked the kindly Buffer.

He replied that he knew enough to distinguish the ship's call sign. But he had hardly settled down in the Asdic chair after the Buffer's departure when the voicepipe marked 'Wardroom' spoke suddenly and made him jump.

'Quartermaster!'

'Sir?'

'Go down, find Michael the Asdic rating and tell him Sub-Lieutenant Sibley wants to see him.'

'Aye, aye, sir.'

He found Michael in the P.O.'s mess with his feet up, reading a detective magazine, and recognised him as the bearded leading-seaman he had seen arguing with the officer when he came on board.

'Well?' said Ernie Michael.

'Sub-Lieutenant Sibley wants to see you in the Wardroom.'

'He does, does he?' said Michael with lowered black eyebrows. 'Well, tell him *if* he does, he can bloody well come down here and see *me*!'

'You're serious?'

'Of course I'm bloody serious, lad. Go on, tell him!'

Thoughtfully Price went back up to his post. He decided to

do nothing and see what happened. A little later the Wardroom voicepipe spoke again.

'Quartermaster! Did you give Michael my message?'

'Yes, sir.'

'Well, why hasn't he come?'

'I don't know, sir.'

There was a short silence. 'Oh, well . . . all right.'

On the messdeck later Price asked about Sub-Lieutenant Sibley and Michael.

'Oh, them – they despise each other.'

'And they need each other. It's their hate that keeps 'em going.'

'Cross-Buckets is the Asdic officer, and he thinks he knows it all.'

'Ernie Michael says that what Sibley knows about the Asdic set wouldn't cover a bloody tram ticket.'

'Ernie's a Regular, see. He doesn't piss about.'

'They're always going at each other hammer and tongs.'

'Aye – when Sibley's not bloody sick.'

'Sick?' said Price.

His listeners looked at him, as if struggling to find words to describe to a newcomer what was exceedingly well known to every other man on board. They were relieved and quickly lost interest when young Eric Brewster took over and explained.

'Mr Sibley suffers badly from seasickness. Really suffers. It starts when we go out and he's sick whenever we hit bad weather. He always keeps a bucket beside him when he's on the bridge. That's how he got his nickname.'

Brewster thought for a while and then added, 'Mr Sibley's not a popular man.'

His quietly considered statement was overheard by a burly seaman who was passing. 'Mr Sibley,' hissed the seaman belligerently, 'is a *bastard*!'

Price was sitting beside the coal fire on the messdeck, watching the dancing flames, when another seaman came over and sat his big frame next to him. Ginger Meeson, an ex-trawler fisherman, was over six feet tall and everything about him was massive; his body, his face, his thick brown arms and hands covered with hair almost down to the knuckles. Price saw a great weatherbeaten face with two deep-set eyes under bushy ginger eyebrows looking hard into his.

'The new hand, eh?'

He nodded.

'I'm just back from sick bay. Had a poisoned finger. It's all right now.' He held up a huge paw as evidence. 'You like being in a trawler?'

'She seems a good ship.'

Ginger studied him, and Price knew that the eyes were calculating that, because he was obviously in his early twenties, his call-up must have been deferred; when he had entered Naval barracks weeks ago the order had already gone out calling up thirty-five-year-olds.

'What did you do in civvy street?'

'I was a bank clerk.'

'Is that right?' said Ginger, deeply interested. 'Matter of fact,' he continued, idly looking up at the bulkhead, 'we had a few bank clerks in my last ship.'

'Did you?'

'Yes, nice fellers – nobody liked 'em. Rotten set of stuck-up bastards we found 'em.'

'You did?'

'Aye. We couldn't stand the boogers. We kicked 'em to death – they were always in and out of sick bay. Had to be done, though. Lousy little nits. Oh well, mate, must be off now – see you later.'

He hoisted up his huge bulk and made off with perfectly straight face.

Later, when the libertymen had returned, Ginger was showing off his card tricks of which he had quite a repertoire. His enormous hands handled the cards with masterful dexterity and he had an expert flow of patter.

'Show him the hair trick, Ginger,' said a seaman, nodding across to Price.

Ginger looked at Price questioningly, and Price, sensing the inevitable, walked across and sat down. A saucer of water was laid on the table. Deftly Ginger plucked a hair from Price's head and laid it on the surface of the water.

'Now then,' Ginger announced, 'by sheer force of electricity I'm going to make that hair stand straight up on end on the water. Watch closely . . . '

Talking all the time and making the job seem one of life and death, he produced a fountain pen, rubbed it hard on his sleeve and brought it close to the hair. Sceptical though he was, Price watched half fascinated under the big man's spell.

'Look, look!' Ginger shouted – 'it's rising up!'

Price craned forward over the saucer to see – and a huge hand came down smack in the middle of it, shooting a shower of water into his face. As the water dribbled from his eyes, his nose, and down his chin he was aware of faces watching him. He smiled, as much at his own gullibility as at the skill of the hoaxer.

Delighted with the success of his trick, Ginger started to laugh and fell back on his bunk, holding his sides. As he continued to laugh, the tone of it became higher and higher until he was shaking and shrieking in a high-pitched falsetto. It was a full minute before he sat up and wiped his streaming eyes.

Eric Brewster caught Price's eye and gave him a wink. Price winked back as he mopped his face with a handkerchief. James, who had come down the messdeck ladder in the middle of Ginger's demonstration, crossed over to Price's bunk.

'You'll do,' he said approvingly. 'Perhaps you *are* too good for a battleship.' He waved a nonchalant good-night and, suddenly grabbing an invisible partner, performed the jerky steps of a tango across to his own bunk with noisy nasal accompaniment.

'Aw, stow it, James.'

He bowed. 'I thank you and good-night, sweet princes all, for tomorrow we're off again to pull old Adolf's nose.'

3

The *Lady Emma* sailed in the afternoon. There was a freshening breeze as she made her way out through the Sound. The big copper spire of Kirkwall's orange stone cathedral faded from sight and all around were snow covered hills. Then they had left the land behind.

Soon the trawler was pitching and bucketing through an uneasy sea. Price developed a splitting headache and felt decidedly giddy.

'Come on, mate, come and have some tea – that'll put you right.'

He had never felt less like having tea, but he went down aft with the others and did his best. Ten minutes later his tea had gone over the side. He crawled into his bunk, leaving it time and again to indulge in another spasm of sickness. Against all advice, he scooped up handfuls of seawater from the swimming deck and drank it; in a curious way it seemed to him the right thing to take. But by nightfall he was in a bad state. They were now well out to sea and the motion increased as the ship wallowed through a heavy swell. She heaved and lurched and groaned and creaked. A sympathetic seaman offered to put a bucket at the side of his bunk, but he refused – he felt it a matter of honour to get out on deck for his bouts.

He lost count of the number of these excursions aloft. It was pitch dark on deck now. The wind had increased and spray was showering across the trawler, which now and again would 'ship it green' amidships, the water swishing about the deck and rushing out through the wash-ports. His stomach had long since emptied, but he still had to go up there and retch and heave, until he thought his very insides would come up under the strain.

At last the need for the constant excursions left him, but by now his insides were so sore it was agony even to move in his bunk. The only position that gave him any relief was to lie flat on his back and, hardly daring to breathe, not move a muscle. He became feverish and was only remotely aware of the ship's alarm-bells clanging, sending all hands scrambling to action-stations. The U-boat alert passed, by which time the fever in him had taken a tight hold and his spells of sleep were filled with monstrous nightmares. He was driving along a precipitous road in his MG Midget swollen to ten times its size. The car's steering jammed, and he shot over the cliff and dropped into a ravine. As he hit the bottom, the steering wheel was driven through his stomach. Or he was being pursued by a horde of Nazis on a wind-swept hillside, his legs dragging like lumps of lead. He rounded a rocky peak and an evil-faced Nazi with fixed bayonet came charging at him and drove the bayonet into his middle. Each time he awoke sweating. He lost all count of time.

At last he saw a face above him, a pleasant, enquiring young face.

'How do you feel, Peter?' asked Eric Brewster.

'Perfectly bloody.'

'The Buffer says to get you up on deck for a spell – it'll do you good.'

Price put on his weather-coat and went shakily up into the cold air. It was broad daylight and all around the crew were at work. Willie Campbell, the Buffer, gave him a rope to coil down, but the bending involved brought on another attack of nausea and he was told to go below again. Brewster brought him a thickly-cut cheese sandwich, but he could not eat it. He went into a semi-coma, and the crash as the vessel hit each new wave seemed to burst in his head.

When he finally came out of it, numbed through all his bones, James said, 'If it's any consolation, Cross-Buckets is still bringing up his insides on the bridge. Sparks, too, has been suffering as usual. He's hardly ever sick, though – stuffs himself with Horlicks tablets, which seem to do the trick. He only goes pea-green.'

Brewster said, 'Bunts has changed his bunk to be nearer Sparks, so I've moved into the bunk above you – if that's all right.'

Price said it was. He didn't blame Bunts for getting well

away from him. He now felt sufficiently recovered to go on deck and do a few odd jobs of seamanship under the guidance of the Buffer, an ex-fisherman from the north of Scotland and one of the most considerate of men. The ship and the guns had to be kept clean, and there was splicing and painting to be done, all the tasks of the daymen of which he was one.

Ginger Meeson watched him at work for a few minutes and then strolled over.

'In my last ship,' said Ginger, 'we had a big, strong bloke who was just bursting to get to sea – all for action and glory, silly sod. We'd not been out more'n a few hours when he took to his bunk – just like you. It was bastard weather, mind you, and the old tub was rolling and pitching like buggery. Well, this lad got worse and worse, and soon he was spewing up blood. Then his mind went twisted and he was right back a kid again. He went up on deck – to spew it up again, we thought – and a deckie just caught him as he was climbing the rail. We had to tie him in his bunk, and he lay there raving. Then he passed right out and we all thought he'd snuffed it. But Jimmy gave him the once-over and reported to the Old Man, and he signalled the convoy S.O. and turned the ship about and we went off back home like the clappers. There was an ambulance all ready waiting on the quay and they rushed him to hospital – just in time. That was the end of Fred for Patrol Service – it was the big ships for him after that, poor bastard.' Ginger belched loudly at the memory then looked Price over thoughtfully. 'You all right now?'

'Yes, thanks.'

But he wasn't. The tender insides of his stomach were trembling again after that story, but he wouldn't show it.

He was given his action-station – as one of the four-inch gun's-crew.

'You're a figures man, I hear,' said 'Guns', the leading-seaman gunlayer, a rotund Yorkshireman. 'So we'll make you sight-setter.'

Within hours they had a practice shoot, during which Price learned that gunnery in a rolling trawler was of the hit-and-miss variety. The task of the *Emma*'s gun's-crew was further complicated by a defect in the trigger mechanism which made the actual moment of firing somewhat uncertain – the shell was equally likely to hit the sea a hundred yards away or go soaring up into the heavens. Guns' language on the subject of the faulty trigger was fruity and to the point.

The remarks of the gunners on the two Hotchkiss machine-guns mounted each side of the bridge also rendered the air purple. For the 'Hotch-*kisses*', as Guns called them, were not liked.

'They're bloody fiddly, inefficient – always jamming. The Lewis gun is far better. We salvaged a lot of these bloody Hotch-*kisses* from the Froggies, and somebody's got to use them but why pick on us?'

The three men on the twin point-five, on its platform aft of the funnel, fared much better, it was a reliable gun. But the session ended with a nasty show of temperament by that incredible machine, the Holman projector. The seaman operating it, having dropped a Mills bomb down the long tube, pressed the pedal, at which the bomb emerged agonisingly slowly from the spout, bobbed up and down on the steam like a ball on a fountain in a fairground shooting gallery, shot up to some twenty feet, fell back on the deck and rolled under the whaleboat.

They all threw themselves flat but, fortunately, the bomb did not explode. Another seaman quickly got to the spot, gingerly retrieved it and swiftly lobbed it far out to sea, where it sank still without exploding. The seaman's great oath of angry relief nearly cleaved the ship. On the bridge Jimmy the One, in spotless white sweater, had watched the scene without moving a muscle, and now turned his back.

'A cool fellow is our Mr Hadley,' said James. 'Now if that bomb had floated over to the bridge . . .'

Later the alarm-bells clanged twice in quick succession, bringing the gun-crews to action-stations. First a merchantman flying the Greek flag was challenged and, on giving satisfactory reply, was 'allowed to proceed', as the bland entry in the *Emma*'s logbook put it. Then a bomber slid over the horizon, flying low. It proved to be British, and the daymen returned to the wire they had been greasing. A Faroese fishing vessel was, out of curiosity, investigated. She had the appearance of a large wooden lifeboat with a small hut erected aft. She was painted red, white and blue, and at the bows bore her number, with the word 'Faroes' on her sides. Her four sails were dull red, the foresail patched with white canvas, and as she slid into a trough, the tops of these were all that were visible. Price felt a fresh twinge in his sorely tried stomach as he watched.

'How are ye feeling?' asked the Buffer.

'I think I'll live.'

'Good. The Cox'n wants me to put you in a watch – we're a mon short.'

'Right.'

A Faroese steam trawler was sighted, challenged and allowed to continue. Then the *Emma* was in turn challenged by a fast and threshing Tribal class destroyer, presumably on her way to escort a convoy. A freak hailstorm advanced like a light mist over the blue-black sea and rattled down on to the deck, stinging the face and tickling the ears and filling the pockets. It was over as swiftly as it had begun, and distant rainfall could be seen hanging all about in the sky in crude daubs of purple and off-white.

Before turning in for his last full night's sleep as a dayman, Price was able to take an interest in the yarning on the benches in front of the messdeck fire. He realised he had not yet seen either the Skipper or the No. 3 officer.

'The Old Man? He's Lieutenant-Commander Ian Lancelot McBride, RNR. "Mac" to you, though not to his face mind.'

'You won't be seeing a lot of him – he leaves handling the crew to Jimmy the One.'

'Aye, and *he*, the snobby booger, leaves it to Cross-Buckets.'

'But Mac's all right.'

'Aye, that he is. Gave oop his little Black Book and went to captain the cross-Channel packets, he did.'

'His Black Book?' asked Price.

'Aw, tell him, Wally,' said a weary voice.

Wally Winters was honest and strong. His face was really ugly, his eyes bulbous, his lips thick, broad and very full, the beard around them matted and fierce. But whenever he spoke, those bulbous eyes came alive. He was a good talker, a raconteur, and it was his expressive eyes that told the story long before the words did. He was as tough and salty as the old *Lady Emma* herself, and was due to go soon for examination for his Mate's Ticket.

'The Black Book, son? Most trawler skippers have them – the pocket books in which they note down, and keep to themselves, their secret knowledge of fish movements gained from year to year.'

'Aye,' broke in another seaman, 'but the book comes second, the nose comes first.'

'True,' said Wally. 'The good skipper can smell out the fish – he doesn't last long if he can't.'

'Some finds it with a prayer and some with a cuss,' said the

23

other seaman. 'Like old Skipper Dan, eh? Tell him, Wally.'

'Skipper Dan,' said Wally obligingly for Price's benefit, 'was your real Aberdeen man. He'd cut a tulip at twenty yards with his spit. Once he burnt his own ship's timbers to get home when the fish forsook him and he ran out of coal round Bear Island. Chopped up all the woodwork they did – what a sight. I wasn't with him that time, but I was on another trip when the trawling gear broke and the nets were rent. He was that fuckin' mad he climbed up to the crow's nest, beat his fists into the wind and cried upon the Almighty, "You grey-haired old bastard!" Aye, a fierce man were old Dan. If the catch were small and without profit, he'd go to his cabin, grab a fistful of silver change and fling it into the sea, crying, "If you won't give us the fish then we'll bloody well *buy it*!" '

'Was Mr Hadley a trawlerman too?' Price asked.

Wally spat into the fire.

'Him? He's R.N.V.R. – a bloody weekend yachtsman!'

When Eric Brewster came off watch Price asked him about the fourth officer.

'Oh, Sub-Lieutenant Grant? He's Signals and Gunnery officer and . . . well, I don't know exactly what else he is, except he and Sparks are always arguing. Nobody takes much notice of Mr Grant.' Brewster looked at Price with a sudden new thought. 'He's not as old as you, you know.'

The talk around the fire was of women and politics and football and films.

'My old woman's got Robert Taylor pinned up beside the bed.'

'You're all right, mate, as long as it's just a picture.'

'Now that Madeleine Carroll, she's a beauty . . .'

'Too posh. Give me the bonnie lassies of Kirkwall any day, you know where you are with them.'

'Aye – nowhere!'

'My girl goes for Clark Gable.'

'Looking at you, Scouse, who'd blame her.'

'We've got our own Clark Gable on the *Emma*.'

'Aye, Jimmy the One. England's answer to Hollywood, that's our Mr Hadley. Leastwise *he* thinks so.'

'Runs through the women like corn, they say.'

'Aye, those bed-and-breakfast Wrens – officers' use only.'

'He never gets his sweater dirty. I've never known him shovel coal.'

'Well, I'd take him any day instead of Cross-Buckets.'

'That two-faced *bastard*!'

The last remark came savagely from the lips of Eddie Nash, a confident and aggressive little Cockney. Eddie was a London tugmaster's son, and what he did not know about the vagaries of the River Thames was not worth knowing. He had a poor opinion of all the officers, the Skipper excepted, and would come down from his watch breathing dire threats of what he would do to them all. Sibley aroused his most scathing anger.

'I'll bleedin' poke him one day, I can't help it. I'll just have to poke him on the nose. Asking me damnfool questions again. First he finds out the answers by asking the Cox'n and then tries 'em on *me*! I told 'im, "Mr Sibley, I don't know and what's more I don't bloody well care, see." "Nash," 'e says, "you're getting far too cocky – you must cut out this cocksure manner of yours." That's when I nearly poked him. Cocksure manner, for Christ's sake! He's an ignorant bastard anyway – always goes by the book. Why, I learnt seamanship on the Thames when he was no more than a twinkle in 'is Dad's eye!'

As Eddie was nearly ten years Sibley's junior, this last observation was a slight overstatement. But, by the book! That was Sibley's culminating crime in the eyes of the lower deck. Anyone who worked 'by the book' was doomed for ever in the trawlermen's estimation. Fishing skippers did not navigate by the book. If they wanted to know where they were, it was said, they just dipped their fingers in the seawater and tasted it. Or they observed what kind of seaweed was floating about.

Eddie, with his mop of flaming red hair, was small, tough and afraid of no one.

'Cross-Buckets,' he declared vigorously, 'should have gorn to a bleedin' battleship. And then Lord 'elp the lot of us!'

One man who did not join in the fireside chatter was Alastair the Stornowegian. Like most men from Stornoway he was quiet, mild and gazed on the world with wondering blue eyes – eyes which had a remarkable range of vision and could see tiny objects at sea even before the officers with their binoculars. Alastair had never before left his native island, and he regarded the conglomeration of men around him with child-like astonishment. His voice had an attractive sing-song note but he talked little, being content to sit over the fire and listen to the babble of tongues. He was deeply religious and always read his Bible before turning in, as Price saw him doing now. Price had often felt Alastair's gaze upon him and looked up to find the round, blue eyes fixed on him with an expression of perplexed amazement. To a Stornowegian, the spectacle of a bank clerk turned sailor must have been strange in the extreme.

Most of the talkers had now dispersed, the only activity being in the after mess, the eating area, where big Ginger Meeson held his nightly solo schools. As he came back from an urgent visit to the juddering Heads, Price passed James, who was already settled in his hammock. James was the only one among them to use a hammock instead of his bunk when at sea. He now lay in his favourite position with the hammock sagging in the middle like a 'V', his bottom almost scraping the deck. He was reading, but looked up at Price and grinned.

'How's your war, Pricey?'

'So-so.'

James saw that his eyes were on the book and raised it up for him to see the title. It was Shakespeare's Cymbeline.

'A little light bedtime culture,' said James.

Eric Brewster lay quiet in the top bunk. Price knew why. Brewster saved up all Enid's letters to him and re-read one of them each day – several times over.

For a moment Price was gripped by a surge of self-pity. There were letters which he now would never receive . . . no letters from home he could reply to and explain his war.

4

The alarm-bells clanged and they tumbled out to their action-stations. It was early morning, dark and very cold.

'Green four five – surface vessel!' bellowed the Skipper from the bridge.

They swung the four-inch round and peered into the darkness. They could just make out a dark smudge on the sea. The *Emma*'s signalman was challenging frantically with his lamp, but there was no answering flash.

'With blank charge, load, load, load!'

They pushed in a blank charge and slammed the breech.

'Fire!'

The explosion nearly lifted them off their feet as the great blastful brute of a gun gave tongue. A shower of sparks went fanning out over the sea.

Still no response. Reload and fire again. They waited, tense.

'With S.A.P., load, load, load!'

A real shell. Here it comes, this was it. Then, from the dark blur, a lamp began to blink.

'Check, check, check!'

Slowly the *Emma*'s signalman interpreted the jerkily delivered reply of the other vessel, which ended with the doleful message 'Lamp – no – good – am – using – torch.' She was a sister trawler of the Northern Patrol.

McBride was furious, and a fierce bout of signalling followed.

'What is your Commanding Officer's name?'

No reply.

'Instruct your Commanding Officer to report on board this ship at daylight.'

'Our C.O. has no intention of leaving his ship.'

'Instruct you to keep a better lookout in future.'

'We keep a perfectly satisfactory lookout.'

'You might have been sunk.'

'By whom?'

And so on. Bob Garrett, the signalman, retailed it all to them later when they were properly awake and thawed out, and could see the funny side of it. In Kirkwall afterwards they would hear the full story. The other signalman's lamp had failed, his spare one was out of action, and he had been running hairless round the ship trying to find a torch. He had found it in the nick of time . . .

It was a busy morning. A convoy had dispersed during the night, either because of inclement weather or the enemy, and the *Lady Emma* sighted, one after the other, three merchant stragglers making for the next place of rendezvous, the custom when a convoy had broken up. Each of the merchantmen was challenged and made satisfactory reply. Later more stragglers passed, all heavily laden, one with planes on her deck, probably from America. Two speedy escort corvettes passed by with them. Then came a destroyer, looking truly splendid in her new camouflage of blue, grey and white, a zig-zag pattern designed to break up her lines so that the enemy could not tell what kind of ship she was. The *Emma* challenged this sleek advertisement for the proper Royal Navy and, in the usual stalwart wording of the log, 'allowed her to proceed'.

Price completed his first four-hour watch. He discovered that the routine consisted of one hour on the bridge verandah facing for'ard, followed by an hour on the boatdeck aft, an hour on the wheel, and an hour as stand-by in the wheelhouse, which involved running errands for the Officer of the Watch, chatting to the man who took over on the wheel, and making 'kye' (cocoa) for the O.O.W., the Asdic rating, the signalman, the telegraphist, and the other men on watch. The wheel was a small one; it worked a steam-driven steering engine and could be easily spun round; but behind it, for use in an emergency, was a large wheel which worked the rudders manually.

The small wheel gave four complete turns in either direction, and the orders for conning the ship were given according to the number of turns required. 'Two turns of port' meant that the wheel would be put half-way over. But ordinary small alterations were given as so many degrees to port or starboard, and this was where the mental arithmetic came in which could cause some men to go through much mental gymnastics and finger-waggling. Price also had to pass on orders to the engine-room by voicepipe and these orders were again given in 'turns'. 'Up ten turns' meaning an increase of ten revolutions in the *Emma*'s reciprocating steam engines, which revolved comparatively slowly.

'It's right, Sam saw a herring-whale following behind us. It must have thought we were fishing!'

Price, as stand-by, had been watching bearded Wally Winters on the wheel, studying his solid dependability and wondering whether he himself would make half as good a sailor as this man going for a Mate's Ticket. Wally was chuckling in his whiskers.

'That whale don't know there's a war on,' he said.

'What *is* a herring-whale?'

'Why, you've heard tell of them, haven't you?'

'I think so,' replied Price vaguely.

'They go begging for fish – begging like a dog.' Wally's eyes brightened in the remembrance of days sailing the free deep seas. 'Wherever you fish for herring it follows the fleet, and as the nets are being hauled it raises its body out of the water, showing a gleaming belly, and takes a good look at what's going on. It isn't timid, no sir, but it's wary. Just like a seal. You throw a herring and it'll catch it. Sometimes one of them will dart towards the ingoing net and snatch a fish neat as a whistle and make off with it. Clever it is, the herring-whale, never been known to rip a net, that skilfully it does its thieving.'

Wally stopped to swig his kye.

'I thought it was the sharks that sometimes got at the nets,' said Price.

'You're right,' said Wally. 'The shark's a thief, but he's a nasty, crude bugger. He'll rip the net and wade in among the fish, grabbing a bit from this fish and a bit from that, spoiling a lot of the catch. Scum of the sea, he is. Not a bit clever, not like your herring-whale.'

In his hour of stand-by on his next watch Price found himself in the wheelhouse with James for company. The Canadian, for that was his nationality, bore little trace of that country's accent due to being born of comfortably off English parents. He stood at the wheel in an attitude of negligent boredom, a cigarette dangling from his lips. His casual responses to the orders from the voicepipe had to be seen and heard to be believed. To a complaint from the bridge he would answer, in hurt tones, 'Sir, I assure you that I am *endeavouring* to comply with your orders ... ' It was remembered by all how the Skipper, beholding James one day in this languid pose, had studied him carefully for a few moments and then gone on his way murmuring, 'And I'll bet he's wearing a wrist-watch ... '

With the cigarette hanging from one side of his mouth James began to hum, with various extra noisy effects, a passage from 'Scheherazade'. Rounding it off with one or two expansive gestures, he announced, 'First Movement, The Sea and Sinbad's Ship. Know it?'

'Yes.'

'Ah, popular stuff.' James stubbed out his cigarette and took a long drink of kye. He was thoughtful for a moment then began to speak quietly and uncharacteristically, without the usual theatricals.

' "The British nation will be considered the most valuable ally in the world, so long as it can be counted on to show that tenacity in its Government as well as in the spirit of the broad masses which enables it to carry through to victory any struggle it once enters on, no matter how long such a struggle may last or however great the sacrifices that may be necessary. And all this, even though the actual equipment at hand may be utterly inadequate when compared with that of other nations." '

He looked at Price inquiringly.

'Churchill?' ventured Price.

'Adolf Hitler. In "Mein Kampf". He's not such a fool.'

Alastair, with his uncanny eyesight, was first to spot the floating mine. The Stornowegian's sing-song warning was echoed through the ship. The *Lady Emma* slewed round and made circuit about it, while all with the inclination went for one of the ship's half a dozen rifles to take a pot-shot at it. The horned menace reeled about on the swelling sea. Round and round the *Emma* steamed and the air was sharp with rifle cracks, the metallic 'chip' of the striking bullet and the high whine of the richochet. Although hit often the mine showed no signs of sinking. The skipper, growing impatient, opened a window of the bridge and took up a rifle himself. Soon afterwards the mine was despatched, but whether by McBride's bullets or those of the Bisley marksmen on deck no one could be sure.

'It's the bleedin' weight of bullets that took it down!' said little Eddie Nash. 'Next time we'd do better getting big Ginger to wrestle it under.'

Ginger Meeson laughed his high falsetto laugh and thought it a huge joke.

Two more ships were challenged, followed by another plane alert. And two more mines were spotted, this time by Sam, the ex-fisherman from Hull. Sam was awarded two packets of ten Woodbines, compliments of the bridge, and the sea was peppered with more bullets from the riflemen, this time producing a more satisfying end result as one of the mines exploded with a roar and a great gout of upsurging, white-whipped sea. It was a sobering thought that this same explosion might have torn and rended an unsuspecting ship's hull. Each one of these lethal objects they disposed of made a safer sea.

Off watch, Price was approached hesitantly by 'Tiny' Carr, one of the stokers, to help him 'wi' ashes'. Already half aware of Tiny's problem, for the unfortunate diminutive stoker was obliged to seek out in turn those seamen disposed to lend him some assistance, Price readily agreed. Tiny had eyes like those of a spaniel and could be very easily wounded.

Pulling up the ashes was the worst part of a stoker's life, which was why it was always performed by a 2nd class stoker. Going out on deck in all weathers, straight from a heated engineroom, it was hard and cold work pulling the heavy bins of ashes up the shaft, lifting them clear and tipping them down the shute into the sea, while the wind blew the grit and ashes into face and eyes. Given the job as the most junior stoker, it was work which Tiny couldn't physically handle by himself, and he was forced to swallow his pride and cadge whatever help the off-duty seamen would give him.

In another vessel Tiny's problem could have been much worse, for there was no love between seamen and stokers, who normally had their own separate messes and lived well apart; but in the *Emma*, with her single communal messdeck, though each faction strongly kept its independence at least most were on speaking terms and sometimes even generous to the point of accepting each other almost as equals. Through helping Tiny, Price was established in the eyes of the stokers. At least, as much as any novice seaman could be. According to Barney, one of the stokers first class, stoking was a job far beyond the brains and muscle of mere seamen. In Barney's opinion it ranked even higher than the job of the signalman or telegraphist. A man could not be a stoker unless he understood coal and heads of steam. The job required the intellect of a Huxley; and as for muscular strength . . . 'You couldn't do it, Pricey. You'd be dead-beat in an hour. What you have to do on deck is nothing to what you have to do in the stokehold. I tell you, it would kill you in a day!'

But from what Price saw going on down in the engineroom it did not look to him as killing as all that. For instead of standing by and feeding the fire frequent small portions of coal, evenly distributed, which would mean staying in the stokehold most of the time, the *Emma*'s stokers piled up large heaps of coal and went back into the engineroom to sit down peacefully and watch the wheels go round – while black smoke billowed forth from the *Emma*'s funnel. Price often looked in to see two or three of the stokers there doing a Mills Brothers act, sitting like birds in a row, singing, their heads nodding in time to the movement of the connecting rods, while the *Emma* streamed betraying smoke heavenwards until the coal burned through.

Prudently he kept well away from the Chief, who watched balefully for any intruder into his domain. The Chief's name was Hook, and some of his more blistering replies up the engineroom voicepipe had become history. He was engaged in continual warfare with the Wardroom and, for that matter, anyone else outside his own jurisdiction. When their paths did cross, Hook stared at Price with a fishy eye, mingling perplexity and censure.

'Ordinary-seaman, eh? Extra-bloody-ordinary seaman I'd call you!'

An embarrassment for Price was the way in which Paddy, a big, softly spoken Irish stoker in his forties, would persist in addressing him as 'Mr Price', a term reserved for officers and not a mere O.D. So Price returned the compliment by addressing him as 'Mr Kelly'. Paddy had no parents, relations or even friends. He was known to spend his leaves living in Service hostels at one and sixpence a night. The rest of his money went on drink. It was, he said, his only pleasure, except – with a twinkle in his bright blue eyes – for a small boy now and again. He boasted of his small boys but no one ever took him seriously. Certainly he had no use for women.

It was grumble time on the messdeck, with the speakers seated defiantly in front of the blazing coal fire. The day's weather had been 'snar'n and blar'n', as Sam the fisherman described it – 'reet lousy,' giving a very chill air and limited atmosphere and visibility combined with great gusts of snow. In such weather, with the decks canting twenty degrees from the horizontal, Sub-Lieutenant Sibley had set men pursuing that most futile of labours, holystoning the deck.

'Bastard!'

'One day I *will* poke him, by God I will.'

'He's going bloody barmy.'

'Aye, the mon's taken leave of his senses.'

'I'll get him, if it's the last thing I do.'

'Steady, lad, or they'll have you chained up in barracks.'

'I'm getting off this stinking old tub.'

They looked with interest at the last speaker. He was Tommy Tilson, a seaman who had been in the Merchant Navy and was inclined to tell endless, boring tales of his travels and of his conquests of women of all nations, none of whom, he swore, could match the Japanese for sheer sexual technique.

'You'll see, this time I'm getting off, I'm going into *submarines*.'

The interest waned. The bee in Tilson's bonnet was his burning desire to leave the *Lady Emma*. He had applied to be a gunner on a merchant ship, a Commando, a paratrooper . . . anything for a draft. But his requests flowed into the Wardroom unavailingly. He was a good hand and the Skipper probably did not want to lose him. Submarines? That, the messdeck decided, wasn't very original.

'What about the Doog?'

'Aye, the poor wee mon.'

'*Mister* Sibley caught him peeling spuds in Jimmy the One's personal dhoby bucket – the one he gets his sweaters washed in. Sibley made Doog paint the ammo boxes on the fiddleys.'

'I'll kill that bleeder.'

Price had seen McDougal miserably doing his painting between gusts of snow. He was a gloomy man of unkempt demeanour with torn rubber boots strapped about his limbs like Anglo-Saxon leggings. He had stubby, scabby hands and his small, thin face teetered on his neck, seemingly burdened by the cap he had fashioned from his balaclava. He wore his oilskin trousers always and, being generally unwashed, had the character of one of the stormers of the Bastille, one of the bread-starved rabble. Like Tilson, he yearned for another ship and was ever discontented.

The weight of melancholy drowned any further bids at conversation, until Sam said, 'Never mind, tea at the "Albert" when we get in.'

James, ambling by Price's bunk, paused to observe, 'Like a

3

Greek chorus, aren't they, dear boy? Oh, woe, woe!'

'What's the "Albert", then?' asked Price.

'The "Albert"? Ah now, how can I find words to express such delight, such heaven, such sheer perfection? It is an oasis in the burning desert, a paradisical port in a savage sea. It is the illusive pool of which we dream, it is our Mecca, the blessed ultimate, the supreme bliss, which keeps us all going through hell and high water on this dreary patrol, until the precious moment when this old kipper smack turns her nose for Kirkwall.' He did a ballet twirl. 'The "Albert",' he said, 'is a tearoom. You'll see.'

As James walked across the messdeck he began to sing, neatly dodging a boot that was flung at him. Big Ginger Meeson, lying on his bunk, tittered hugely, then joined in the song with his fog-horn voice.

'Some – where . . . o – ver the rain – bow . . .'

James Crawford was both a mystery and a source of continual amusement to the rest of the crew. He had come over from Canada to join up and had been with the *Lady Emma* for ten months. *Ten months.* Ten months on Northern Patrol – the thought to Price, at that moment, was a daunting one. James – no one ever called him 'Jim' or 'Jimmy' – had such obvious talents and, beneath his casual veneer, a certain strength and resilience – he could more than pull his weight with any man. Yet he was still just a seaman, content to spout his poetry in bed and declaim Shakespeare with dramatic intensity, his general manner of speech leaving most of the crew flabbergasted. He never swore, but would abuse his mockers with long words foreign to their ears. As one bemused stoker had explained to Price, 'I told James to get stuffed and he came back at me with a bleedin' word this long' – and he held out his black hands about four feet apart.

'A broken-down toff,' Ginger Meeson called James. 'You irresponsible piece of inadequacy,' James threw back at Ginger, at which the big man dissolved into peals of laughter.

James's virtue was that he could take it. Price wondered whether he would reach that enviable stage.

The wind, blowing from the north, freshened into gale force, whipping the crests off the tops of the waves and sending clouds of icy spray scudding over the ship. It cut into the faces of the lookouts until they assumed the colour of raw steak.

'Clear lower deck! All hands on top!'

The cry brought them clumping out of the hatch, shivering as they met the impact of the freezing gale. Price saw that the whaleboat had broken adrift and was swinging free on its davits, lashing and crashing into everything around it. While the *Emma* was brought round in the teeth of the gale to give them a lee in which to work, they all heaved and struggled and fought to bring the rampaging brute under control, Price and some others almost up to their waists in water as they worked.

He found himself next to Sub-Lieutenant Grant, the young No. 3, who besides making encouraging shouts was pitting his strength with the rest of them. The other two officers, Hadley and Sibley, each seemed to be shouting different orders. Chaos reigned supreme. Big Ginger had ideas of his own as to how things should be done and even in the gale his megaphone-like voice drowned the rest. There was a sudden desperate cry not far away from Price as a great burst of sea surged over and swamped them, and when he shook the water from his eyes and looked across he saw Sibley suspended half over the ship's side and half over the angry sea. For a frozen moment in time the scene was sharply etched. Sibley's groping arms, his wide open mouth and frightened eyes – and the look on the face of the seaman nearest to him. It was Eddie Nash. The little Cockney's teeth were bared, his jaw thrust out, the lips curled back in sneering contempt and the light of hatred in his eyes. It could only have been for a fraction of a second that he stared at the helpless officer with utter loathing. Then he had grabbed Sibley's leg and roughly yanked him down to fall with a splash to safety in the swirling mess on deck.

A piece of loose timber struck Price on the head and, temporarily dazed, he clung on to a rope. Then he was aware that McBride had arrived on the scene. The Skipper had been turning the ship round. Now, perched perilously on the boat platform close to the whaleboat's lashing hull he brought order out of dangerous confusion with a few calm commands and gestures. In a short time the errant boat was secured again.

The gale raged all through the night, buffeting the ship with its great icy blasts and lashing the sea to a frenzy.

James, looking across from his swaying hammock, quoted, ' "Give me a spirit that on this life's rough sea, loves t'have his sails filled with a lusty wind . . . " How's your head, Pricey?'

'Sore.'

'Cheer up, scout – the worst is yet to come.'

5

Oh, happy day! The engineroom telegraph rang 'Full-ahead' and the *Lady Emma*, breaking out of her slow, somnambulistic patrol speed set her bows for Kirkwall at her heroic best speed of nearly ten knots. On the messdeck the subject which dwarfed all others was that of a refit.

'Dosta think we'll go down to G.Y. this time?'

'Not a chance, we won't see Grimsby yet awhile. You know we haven't done six months on patrol yet.'

'Aye, but we've had the boiler trouble.'

'No chance. The Chief soon patched it up.'

'That's reet.'

'I wish they'd put me on that job – *I'd* have seen to the boiler!'

'Won't be G.Y. this time – next time maybe,' Bunts observed without looking up from the magazine he was reading.

'Why, any buzzes in the signals, Bunts?'

'No – just my guess.'

'You bleedin' old flag-wagger – ain't you got a home to go to?'

'What about you, Sparks?'

'Nothing at all, chum. If I knew anything I'd tell you. Straight up.'

'Jerry – any talk in the Wardroom?'

The young curly-haired seaman-steward who served the officers and prided himself on having the ear of the Skipper regretfully shook his head.

'No. I don't think they know any more than we do.'

'Ah well, live in hope, lads.'

'Don't suppose we'll know for sure till we're coaling.'

In the heavy silence that followed Price said he didn't understand what coaling had to do with it.

'Look, lad, if doo goes to collier for a hundred and sixty tons of coal, den it means another bastard patrol. But if doo finds doos only got seventy tons, dat means G.Y. and up the line. See?'

'Bunts, keep your eyes skinned for the coaling signal when we get in – and none of your bleedin' hush-hush stuff!'

James, who had taken no part in the discussion but sat with his ear glued to the messdeck wireless, waved them quiet.

'Enough of speculation!' he shouted. 'Here's Bebe Daniels and Vic Oliver.'

As 'Hi, Gang!' was a very popular programme with them all the thorny topic was dropped and they gathered round the set, which was working well again now they were in closer home waters. They listened, content at least that they were bound for Kirkwall, beer and letters; each man silently promising himself a feast of sausages and chips, and the more optimistic a steak.

The *Emma*'s engines throbbed purposefully, vibrating through the ship as she made her way homewards. The going had turned rough again with a long sea which was truly mountainous. One moment she would be climbing painfully up a blue-black hillside; then she would be descending into a forbidding valley. But this sort of sea suited the trawler better than a short sea; it gave a steadier movement, without the violent bucketing and crashing which flung cursing men from one end of the messdeck to the other and back again before they had recovered.

The *Lady Emma* steamed into the calmness of Kirkwall harbour in the early morning light and made straight for the collier. Signalman Garrett came down from the bridge to find all eyes fixed on him expectantly.

'A hundred and sixty tons,' he said briefly.

Amid a dead silence, Jerry the steward pulled down his suitcases, which he had been carefully packing for the past week, and began to remove the contents.

'They'd keep this bloody old wreck sailing if she was held together with string!' said a disgruntled voice. But it was a rather desperate exaggeration and they all knew it. The *Emma* might do another two or three patrols before her turn for a refit came up, and with it their leave; only no man liked to dwell upon that.

As the work of coaling up started the wind whipped coaldust into the eyes and throats of the men and some used their gasmask eyeshields in an attempt at protection. As the collier's great grabs opened their jaws and crashed the coal down on the *Emma*'s deck the men shovelled it away to the bunkers like navvies. For a time Price worked in a coalhole with Geordie, who was in savage mood and further inflamed by Price's inexperience and occasional wild struggles with the shovel.

'Ah, but you're worse than our Maggie!'

Geordie was a dangerous man. Unlike big Ginger, whose massive paw could crush a man but who had never been known to use his great strength in anger, Geordie was a fighter who lusted for blood, be it his opponent's or his own that was ultimately spilled. He would use his head, knees, elbows, anything, in a scrap; there was no Queensberry rules nonsense about him. He had worked in the Durham pits, where men were men and fights were murder. 'Where I come from,' he would shrill, 'we kill men – aye, we kill 'em all right!' But, although keeping a wary eye out, nobody took this kind of threat very seriously. If they had been serious, the ship would have been several officers short, for Geordie was frequently to be heard plotting their deaths.

'Yon bastard will never see yam again after this trip,' he would mutter darkly. 'He'll go over the side with my foot behind him – you'll see.' But somehow, the officer would get 'yam' after all.

Now, Geordie vengefully tackled each shovelful of coal as if it were an officer – and banged and crashed and snuffed the life out of it. After a time Price became detached from Geordie and was shovelling away industriously, and a little more expertly, when he suddenly realised who was now working beside him – the Skipper. McBride, in old clothes, with eyebrows bristling and weatherbeaten nose snorting in the flying dust, was also shovelling coal down into the insatiable maws of the bunkers. Price warmed to the Skipper's vigorous example. Elsewhere young Sub-Lieutenant Grant seemed to be enjoying himself hopping in and out of the bunkers wielding a useful shovel. Sub-Lieutenant Sibley, too, was actually working a shovel when not pausing to issue curt advice to those around him. Only Lieutenant Hadley was not seen to lift a shovel-load, being loftily engaged in administrative duties, his sole contribution to the hard, sweaty work going on around him consisting of a few sarcastic observations on sailors and shovels.

James, using his shovel extravagantly, sometimes as a knight's lance to spear a squirming foe, sometimes as a fish-shop scoop to serve up 'Cod and two penn'orth, ducks,' watched Hadley with a grimy eye.

'Methinks Johannes the First liketh not the homely toil.'

There was a lively diversion when a Signals Office messenger arrived on board with confidential orders 'for the C.O. only'.

'Right,' said McBride brusquely. 'Let's have them.'

The messenger eyed the Skipper, in his old clothes and smothered in coaldust like the rest, and gave him a withering glare.

'I want the C.O., matey,' he said.

McBride slapped his shovel down with a clang, stood up to his full five feet ten inches in the middle of the deck and roared, 'Steward! Fetch me my bloody cap!'

When Jerry Baxter arrived with it on the double, McBride clamped it on his head and, with eyes blazing, held out his hand.

'Now! Hand over my orders, sailor!'

The messenger nervously passed over the envelope, saluted frenziedly with enough force to break his arm, and slunk away as cowed and unclean as a pariah dog.

They coaled throughout the day, with breaks, till their breath came frostily on the chill evening air. The job done, the *Emma* moved off to moor at a buoy. Now they could rest from their labours and half the crew could look forward to the joys of Kirkwall tomorrow, as the libertymen took it in turns to go ashore.

But first, the mail. Word had gone round the ship that a drifter had delivered mail to the Wardroom, where the officers sorted out their own letters first. Then down the messdeck hatch came the welcome shout, 'Mail coming below!' Everyone waited with ill-concealed expectancy. Then down the ladder came a seaman with the sack which he emptied on to a table, Eddie Nash being elected to dole out the letters.

Among the mail were local newspapers, magazines, and a few small parcels of comforts. Soon the lucky recipients of these were proudly displaying their scarves, socks and jerseys.

Some men took their letters to their bunks to lie and read in silence, others were pleased to deliver their domestic news to all and sundry.

'Listen to this ... our Winnie's getting wed ...'

'My old lady's got 'erself a war job ...'

'Our cat's had kittens ...'

'My brother's been home on leave from Scotland . . . '

Big Ginger read his one letter in silence, stuffed it into a pocket, collapsed on his bunk, belched loudly and began to sing. He never wrote his wife a line from one leave to the next, but he considered this quite in order. So long as he turned up safely every seven months or so with a fat pay packet he was doing his duty.

Swanson, one of the Asdic operators, complained bitterly as usual about his wife writing to him only once a month. He himself wrote regularly, marking the backs of the envelopes with S.W.A.L.K. and other endearing symbols. It was a sentimental touch that went curiously with the rest of his character, for Swanson was jumpy and eccentric – and so was his Asdic companion, Jones. The general opinion was that all Asdic men ultimately went crazy and that Swanson and Jones were three parts there already. Unlike Ernie Michael, the senior Asdic man, who, although in constant argument with Cross-Buckets, kept his feet solidly on the deck, seemingly unaffected by the monotonous 'ping-ping' of his infernal submarine detector. 'Little Sir Echo, how do you do . . . ' he would croon happily through his beard while taking part of the set to bits.

'Well,' said Eddie Nash, 'that's it, we've had the lot.'

Some of those who had not received letters allowed themselves to be coaxed into reading those of their mates.

Price re-read the letter from his sister.

'I gave the rest of Dad's clothes to the W.V.S. . . . If you really want the watch, of course you may have it . . . Harry says you *must* come to stay with us when you get leave . . . Please . . . '

He felt a great emptiness well up inside him.

'Good news?' said Brewster encouragingly, looking down from the top bunk with a friendly smile. He had been enjoying a feast of news from Enid, his eyes lingering over each loving sentence, the feel of the coloured notepaper and its suggestion of female fragrance adding to his inner excitement.

James burst into sudden voice.

'A Salvation Army lass,
Thought she heard an ass,
Singing Alleluia,
How peculiar!'

'Aw, get stuffed, James.'

'Courtesy of "Men Only", chaps.'

'Get back to bleedin' Shakespeare.'

'Thank you. I thank you, one and all.'

40

When the swapping of family news had subsided, the talk round the messdeck fire turned to boxing and women, and travel and women, and fishing and women, till one by one they sought their bunks.

It snowed during the night. The next day broke heavily slushy, with all hands on the *Lady Emma* moving with mincing steps like so many Chinese over the slippery decks. Some men suffered the indignity of falling and collecting a bruise with the *Emma* not even in motion. But when big Ginger slipped and fell he just lay there and laughed, while the ship trembled as if she were the bruised party.

'Price! Wanted in the Wardroom!' called the Quartermaster from above.

He arrived at the holy-of-holies to find the trawler's whole quartet of officers present. The gin bottle was out, and McBride's craggy face had a look of mischievous geniality about it. Jimmy the One lounged as was his manner in an impeccable white sweater, while Sibley and Grant were more formally attired and clearly wary of the Skipper's eye. On the table, at McBride's elbow, were several papers, on one of which Price could read his own name and Service number. So this was the famous White Paper of a C.W. candidate.

'Price, I see ye are in for a commission,' said McBride.

'Yes, sir.'

'And how are ye getting on? Learning a bit?'

'A bit, sir.'

'I hear the sea put ye to your bunk!'

Price flushed.

'Have ye not been to sea before, laddie?'

'No, sir. That is, except for a Mediterranean cruise.'

'A cruise, is it?' McBride's eyes showed their amused surprise. 'And what kind of a sailor were ye then?'

'I don't think I was sick.'

'No, in a *cruise* ship I don't suppose ye would be. I see your call-up was deferred.'

'Yes, sir.'

McBride waited. So did Sibley and Grant. Price screwed himself up to finding the words.

'My father . . . was dying. I had to look after him.'

'Och, laddie. Have ye no family?'

'A married sister, sir.'

'How are ye on the wheel?' McBride looked across at Sibley,

41

who nodded. 'Ye know, laddie, there's no room in a trawler for officer-training.'

'No, sir.'

'But Mr Sibley will keep an eye on ye.'

'Thank you, sir.'

'What made ye volunteer for the Patrol Service, Price? Was it torpedo *speed*boats ye were thinking of, mebbe?' he asked with heavy humour.

'No, sir. I had a rough idea of what to expect.'

'Ye did? Ye divil! All right, Price, that'll be all.' McBride gave a kindly nod and added, 'I see ye can handle a shovel.'

Price returned to the messdeck to find Tommy Tilson and Eddie Nash, who had both preceded him to the Wardroom, holding forth to a knot of interested listeners. Tilson was complaining loudly. His application to be drafted to the submarine service had been duly put before McBride, but even before it was sped on its way Tilson knew from his interview that the Skipper would not give it its required recommendation.

'I'll get him,' Tilson promised grimly. 'I'll get old Mac yet. I'll find a way off this bloody boat – you just see if I don't!'

Eddie Nash was whitefaced and so worked up inside that he could not stop the corners of his mouth from twitching.

'Cross-Buckets thanked me,' he said. 'In front of the Old Man. He *thanked* me. The rotten bastard . . . ' The words dribbled away, he was too choked to say any more. To be thanked for saving his arch-enemy in the storm was too much to bear. Once again, in bringing the incident into the open, Sibley had sadly misjudged his man. Had he spoken privately to Eddie, or better still let the incident ride, he might have been credited with an ounce of common sense. But now . . .

'How did *you* get on with dear old Mac?' James asked Price. 'Did he offer to make a mon of ye? He did me. Who do you reckon's winning?'

Price smiled, but gave no answer.

In the afternoon the busy drifter which had called earlier with the 'Chippies' to repair the whaleboat now came to take the libertymen ashore. Price and Brewster had planned to explore the delights of Kirkwall together, but Brewster had since been put down for a turn as Quartermaster, so James very generously volunteered his company.

Now the mysteries of the 'Albert' were revealed. It was a pleasure for which one had to queue in the slush – but willingly, the Navy and Army united in the common bond of stomach love. A notice hanging in front of the cretonne curtains of the tearoom announced the opening time of four o'clock, and eagerly the queue of sailors and soldiers awaited the drawing back of the curtains which heralded the opening of the door. The parting of the curtains disclosed the scene within: the polished red panelling, the cheerful, wide hearth, the blue china and bright brass on the wall-ledge, and the tables – stiff white linen, willow-pattern cups and plates, rich yellow butter-pats, fresh bread stacked high, fresh bronzed scones, luscious velvet pancakes, and cakes in paper cups. With the opening of the door a fortnight's dream came true. All went in with a rush to grab tables, but once they were seated the air of decorum returned. Every rating and every 'squaddie' was on his best behaviour at the 'Albert'.

'Well?' said James, when the tastes of crisp new scones and buttered flapjacks thick with strawberry jam were still on their lips.

'Excellent,' said Price.

' "Jack's" pleasures are very simple, dear boy. But d'lovely.'

They went shopping in the ancient town's narrow streets and James bought some second-hand books. They queued for beer, then paid their ninepences at the picturehouse and saw a Deanna Durbin film; James was a great movie fan and actually kept quiet throughout the show. Afterwards they had to rush for the drifter, but found time to dash into a fish-shop for sausages and chips which they ate as they hurried shivering through the cold night.

Returned to the *Lady Emma*, the libertymen sought to spread their conviviality among those who had remained on board – especially the ones who had gone diligently seeking beer. And it required diligence, for the pubs of Kirkwall only opened for an hour or two each night and men had to queue, dash to a table with their drink, then quickly queue again for another. Some went round like this in an endless queue, downing their hard-won collection of drinks in the mad last minutes.

Ginger Meeson settled to a demonstration of his card tricks, finding great scope in the person of a new stoker who had joined the ship to replace one who had gone off to sick bay with grinding stomach ulcers. The new man was from Grimsby, a big lad and gawky. Ginger switched the fun to a display of one of his famous 'scientific' tricks. Standing away from the table he pushed a funnel down the front of his trousers, held back his head and carefully placed a penny on his forehead. Then, with a

43

great show of precision and skill, like a balancer in a circus, he inclined his head forward until the coin fell neatly into the funnel.

'I bet,' said Ginger, 'you can't do that.'

Innocently accepting the challenge, 'Grimmy' stood up and slowly and seriously positioned himself with the funnel stuck in his belt. While his head was held back studiously balancing the penny, a jug of water was speedily produced and Ginger adroitly poured it into the funnel, filling the stoker's trousers. Then he flung himself on his bunk and began shrieking his girlish peals of laughter, when to his surprise the victim went white with rage and flung himself on Ginger, fists flying. Ginger continued to howl in a falsetto of mirth, but on receiving a few hearty punches from the enraged newcomer he had to take action. He did not fight back but, helped by others, he pinioned 'Grimmy's' arms and held him down until his anger had subsided, for one retaliatory blow from Ginger's leg of mutton fist would have done the man serious harm.

Paddy the stoker came back on board looking the worse for wear. One eye was purple and his lips were cut.

'Hello, boys, how are you all?'

'All right, Paddy, and how's yourself?'

'Fine, me bhoy, nivver better.'

No one made any mention of his appearance; that was a thing they never did. He walked round the bunks, talking to each of them, and they replied normally, as if nothing was amiss.

'Are you happy, Mr Price?'

'Yes, Mr Kelly, I am.'

Paddy seated himself on a bench in front of the fire and began to croon, 'Oh, Mary, this London's a wonderful sight . . . ' Gradually his body drooped further and further forward, until he suddenly collapsed in a heap on the deck. Four of them lifted him up and deposited him in his top bunk.

In the morning they got to know the story.

'Paddy ended up in a scrap with two buggers from the *King Richard*.'

'That shitty old Fleetwood boat!'

'They were lucky not to get picked up, all of them.'

'What were they fighting about?'

'Oh, the usual.'

The 'usual' was the sore topic of Southern Ireland's continued neutrality in the war, which, denying bases for the British, allowed German ships, and more particularly U-boats, to sail those coasts with impunity.

'Oh, Ulstermen, eh?'

'No, southern Irish, same as Paddy.'

Eddie Nash spat into the fire in disgust.

'The Irish don't make bleedin' sense,' he said. 'None of 'em. Fighting each other – and they're already in the war! They're like big bloody children.'

'Shall we be telling that to Paddy, now, Eddie?'

'I don't care a fish's tit what you do.'

'Have you heard about the *Ocean Crystal*?' said another voice.

'No.'

'T'other night the crew heard the sound of a shot. "Ah," they said – "old Jimmy's shot his bloody self." And would you believe it, next day they found that he *had*. Put a bullet through his head. And just as he was about to go on twenty-eight days' leave, too!'

All fell silent in shocked astonishment. If the trawler's No. 1 had just returned from leave, shooting himself would have made good sense. But *before* going on leave – incredible!

'I bet the poor sod had turned religious,' said Eddie Nash. Then he caught Alastair's blue eyes staring at him. The Stornowegian had just tucked his Bible under his pillow; he never slept without it there.

Eddie went up on deck. It had snowed luxuriously and now the sun shone. Kirkwall Bay was unusually calm, the visiting drifters not even ruffling the surface of the water as they passed.

'Doin' the Lambeth Walk – *oi*!' shouted a figure by the funnel.

'Aw, knock it off, James – we're not all bleedin' pearly kings.'

James went ashore with the storeboat and returned with a large, mysterious object wrapped in a canvas bag. That night he opened the bag to display a gramophone and a dozen records.

'To replace the one that took a walk – and steady as you wind it up, gentlemen, it's a mite fragile. There's Harry Roy and Bing Crosby – and Wagner and Tchaikovsky . . .'

Groans.

'Mac's back on board, lads,' came the shout.

'Good,' said James, carefully inspecting his tobacco tin full of gramophone needles. 'Now at least we have a driver.'

They sailed the following day at noon, and with the order 'Ring down slow speed' the *Lady Emma* resumed her solitary beat.

6

The big merchant ship sighted by the *Lady Emma* when challenged turned out to be Swedish, and gave her destination as Thorshaven. But on being allowed to proceed she unexpectedly steamed away on a completely contrary course. McBride's suspicions were aroused and the *Emma* put on speed to intercept.

'Gun-crew close up!'

They waited.

'With blank charge, load, load, load!'

They waited again.

'Fire!'

With a thunderous detonation the *Emma* showed her teeth, but the blank shell gave off a nauseating odour that hung about the gun-crew in a bilious cloud and made them cough. To their relief the 'suspect' ship stopped and, ordered imperiously by McBride to send over a boat, did so, a beautifully painted boat as pristine as an illustration in a shipping company's glossy brochure. Lieutenant Hadley, dashing in his white sweater and officer's half boots, climbed down into it and was taken across the calm stretch of sea to have words with the erratic Swede's captain.

'There goes Clark Gable the second,' said Eddie Nash. 'He only needs a bleedin' cutlass and he'd show 'em!'

Price watched the No. 1 make the crossing. Hadley certainly looked a brisk and efficient embodiment of the Royal Navy, weekend yachtsman though he might be. The *Emma* steamed around for nearly half an hour awaiting his return. When the boat reappeared he was laughing and joking with the merchant officer in charge of it; all was well. He climbed jauntily back on board the *Emma*, the boat returned to its mother ship and the Swede continued on her way.

Eric Brewster had come up on deck for air, looking very green about the gills.

'How are you doing?' asked Price.

'Oh, I'll get the hang of it, I suppose.'

Brewster had been appointed messman for the duration of the patrol, a hard job which involved assisting the cook by serving up the food to the crew, two sittings for every meal, and cleaning all the pots and pans.

'Can I help you with anything?'

'No, thanks, I'll manage,' said Brewster stoically. Soon he had gone below again to resume his fragile liaison with the unpredictable cook.

Price was feeling well pleased with himself. His stomach had more or less righted itself within hours of the *Emma* leaving Kirkwall and this time he had been able to savour the breaks in the weather and see more of what was going on; unlike Sparks, who was still on a diet of Horlicks tablets, and Sub-Lieutenant Sibley, who never strayed far from his sick bucket on the bridge. Two more ships were challenged with much less fuss than had attended the wayward Swede, and they also sighted the familiar dried-blood red of Faroese fishing sails, replete in the wind like the distended stomachs of puppy-dogs.

Sharp-eyed Alastair spotted a loose mine bobbing in the far distance and collected his prize of ten Woodbines, the Skipper's standing reward for such vigilance. Alastair did not smoke, and what he did with his hoard of cigarettes no one had ever found out. Eventually they all saw the mine, floating like a monster poppy-head. It was a British mine of the type which was supposed to render itself safe on coming adrift from the minefield, but the rule was that the only safe mine was a sunken one, and so the marksmen got busy and it was despatched in a matter of eight rounds.

That night Price was on for'ard lookout, with Sub-Lieutenant Grant as officer of the watch. The night sea was passive, allowing the *Emma* to glide through the rippling waves. Out of the corner of an eye Price saw the young officer studying him through the bridge window. Then he was out beside him on the bridge verandah.

'Price!'

'Sir?'

'Here's a question for you. If you were O.O.W. and you saw a green light to starboard, what would you do?'

'Nothing, sir.'

'Why not?'

'Because it would be another ship's starboard light going in the opposite direction. *"If on your starboard hand is seen, a steamer's steaming light of green, there's nothing much for you to do, as green to green keeps clear of you."* '

Grant chuckled, Price thought with some relief, as if the ice between them were broken. The embarrassing age gap, Grant being nearly two years younger than he, seemed to recede a little, and with it momentarily the barrier between officer and rating.

'Ah,' said Grant, 'you have been studying those little rhymes! Well done, they come in very handy.'

'Yes, sir.'

'What would you do if your engines broke down at sea?'

'Hoist two black balls, meaning "Not under command".'

'Good. What about at night?'

'Two red lights, one above the other.'

'Right. What lights does a vessel under way carry?'

'A white light on the mainmast facing for'ard and ten points of the compass either side, a green light to starboard and a red light to port.'

'Right again. If you saw a vessel with one or two white lights visible all round the horizon, what would she be doing?'

'She'd be at anchor.'

'Good, you seem to know your lights, but of course in wartime we can rarely show any – which makes things difficult.'

'Yes, sir.'

Grant, warming to his little quiz, suddenly flung out an arm.

'You are entering harbour and see a conical-shaped buoy. What do you do?'

'Leave it on my starboard hand.'

'And a can-shaped one?'

'Leave it to port.'

'And a spherical buoy?'

'Means you can pass it on either side.'

'Good. Keep at it.'

'Yes, sir.'

Grant returned to the bridge-house, well satisfied with the outcome of his interrogatory session on the Seamanship Manual.

Iceland's influence became apparent a good eight hours before the island was actually sighted, for the wind off its snow-covered peaks was chill, and reached them at midnight, whereas they did not come upon the island till eight o'clock in the morning. Iceland! They were on the most northerly line of patrol. They could see the magnificent slopes of Hekla and the attendant ranges. Their view of Iceland took in a quarter of the compass, from the stupendous grace of Hekla declining into lesser prominences to the east, all jagged and sharp with deep shadows and blinding whiteness.

'In very truth, moon mountains!' said James, with as much fresh enthusiasm as if he were seeing them for the first time. 'I hear you soon got your sea-legs this time.'

'I'm improving, I think.'

'Mr Sibley's on the warpath between visits to his sick bucket. He's had an almighty row with Ernie Michael and has "bottled" Tommy Tilson and the great unwashed McDougal. Everything proceeds as normal, cap'n. The Chief is muttering fearful oaths about his engines and Tiny Carr's looking for help "wi' ashes", I'm going down to play some records. Coming?'

'Later,' said Price. He wanted to watch the Icelandic coast a little longer. When he finally went down to the messdeck Tilson was in full voice, announcing that he had decided to volunteer for the Tank Corps.

'I know a good bit about engines, see – *that's* in my docs,' he said defiantly. 'The Old Man can't deny that.'

'What about a job with the Chief, then? He'd love to have you down in his engineroom.'

Tilson looked murderously at the speaker. 'I could do *his* bloody job right enough,' he said. 'I could paddle this old bathtub to Honolulu and back!'

'That's your trouble, Tommy – you're too good a sailor. That's why Mac doesn't want to lose you.'

'He'll lose me right enough. I *promise* you.'

'Look out, those Nazi tanks,' said a dry voice.

Tilson went off to his bunk, scowling at James who was energetically conducting the orchestra as he played Harry Roy's noisy record of 'Somebody Stole My Gal'.

Price found Brewster lying quiet in his top bunk, snatching a respite from his mess duties to re-read a letter from Enid.

'All right now?'

'A touch of stomach cramp, I think,' said Brewster reluctantly. 'It's all that food, the smell. It gets a hold of you.'

49

'Try not to think about it – just look on it as another job.'

'Yes – I'll try.'

The *Lady Emma* rode a mountainous sea, climbing the cresting waters and gliding into the grey-green depths. The waves were powerful 15-footers. Occasionally the sea slapped the beam and the *Emma* staggered, gasped, paused, then was again resolute to the task. The weather grew colder and heavier and the ship's bows gouged the waters, shooting monstrous plumes of ice-green spray on either side, spray which gusted against the bridge windows like rain and made crossing the open deck from the shelter of the bridge to the foc's'le companionway a game of skill and daring if one was to avoid a drenching. Some dashed the distance and chanced that speed would outwit weather. Others moved Apache-wise from cover to cover with ever an eye for that momentary lull.

In the early light of a cold dawn Alastair's cry on lookout of, 'Submarine off the port bow!' was heard and quickly repeated throughout the ship. The *Emma* went to full speed with her crew at action-stations. Was this it?

'With S.A.P. load, load, load!'

On the bridge McBride's binoculars probed the area of sea where Alastair had spotted a submarine's periscope protruding above the surface of the water. Suddenly it was plainly discernible, then – 'Check, check, check!'

As the *Emma* drew closer they saw that the 'periscope' was in fact the bobbing, empty mast of a ship's smallboat. All eyes strained to spot some sign of life in the boat, but there was none. It could be a trap, for loose boats and rafts were known to have been used as 'bait' by the enemy to lure an unsuspecting ship within range of the torpedoes of a lurking U-boat. So the *Emma* went in cautiously, every gunner at nervous readiness, but the 'pinging' of the Asdic was clean and clear. When she came alongside the boat Price and Ginger Meeson were ordered to search it under the coolly watchful eye of Lieutenant Hadley. The boat bore the name of the s.s. *Vega*, a Norwegian. It had been damaged on one side as if launched in a hurry, but the only signs of late human occupancy were a rumpled thick blue sweater and a single seaboot stocking. They investigated the boat's water barrel, which was full, then handed up its store of biscuits, flares and matches.

'The boat's food rations are incomplete,' said Lieutenant Hadley as he made some notes, then ordered the plug to be taken out and the boat was pushed off and allowed to sink.

What had happened to the *Vega*? Signals went off to Base telling of the *Emma*'s discovery, but no information was forthcoming in return.

'Come on, Sparks, what's going on?'

Telegraphist Tom Knox spread out his hands and shrugged.

'Don't ask me. There's some talk of a raider in these waters – but nobody knows who or what. There's a U-boat alert out. But maybe the *Vega* simply lost her boat?'

'Maybe,' said Wally Winters reflectively. 'But it's not likely. You don't hang or launch a boat with her mast up.'

'They could have launched the boat, put up the mast, then left it in a hurry – perhaps the *Vega* was hit but didn't sink, so they went back to her. That kind of thing does happen.'

'Aye.'

It was a feasible explanation, but there were other theories on the tips of a dozen tongues as a *Marie Celeste* mystery threatened to assert itself. Only the spotting of two more mines put paid to further speculative discussion. One was seen by Alastair, the other by Ted Beckles. The rifle party let fly and were rewarded with two considerable explosions, but somehow there was not the same enthusiasm for this familiar sideshow after the haunting discovery of the empty boat. Somewhere, were shipwrecked men struggling against the sea? Evidently McBride had decided that a search would be fruitless.

When on stand-by with James at the wheel, Price asked, 'Has the *Emma* ever found a U-boat?'

'In my time, two or three,' replied James casually. 'Twice when we were doing sweeps with the *Ocean Crystal*. But on each occasion, as soon as we got a firm contact on Jerry's tail we trawlers were told to clear off and leave the job to the real Navy – destroyers. They don't trust us, you see, old boy. And why should they? A U-boat on the surface can do double our best ten knots.'

'You've seen one?'

'Yes. The one we found all by ourselves. As soon as we got the old "ping-ping . . . ping-ping" Trotters was off.'

'Trotters?'

'Trotman – our old C.O. before McBride. Hardly ever saw a sober day, that man, used to go to bed with a bottle, but he was a brilliant sailor. He took us haring after that U-boat like a dog after a rabbit. But do you know what happened?' James spiralled the cigarette held loosely between his lips. 'Up came that cheeky Jerry – surfaced miles away and just cruised off, showing us a clean pair of heels and the old "Up you, mate" I've no doubt.'

'He escaped?'

'Yes, old boy. On the other hand,' James added thoughtfully, 'you might say *we* did.'

'Why didn't the U-boat attack?'

'You'll have to ask the Wardroom questions like that, Peter Price. Especially if you're thinking of joining it. However, as you seek the benefit of my infinite wisdom, I'll tell you – the old *Emma*'s not really much of a catch for a U-boat, is she? Not worth a Jerry kapitan's expensive torpedo. It's the supply ships and warships they're after.'

'You mean they just ignore our trawlers?'

'Sometimes they do – sometimes they don't. The trawler *Derryman* went down near here. She was riding along doing nobody any harm when a surfaced U-boat stole up behind her and raked her with its big gun. She blew up. Seventeen men were saved, less than half the crew. You've heard the saying, "It isn't where you've been that matters, it's where you're going"? Well, it isn't true, they found that out on the *Derryman*. And the moral of this little tale is, keep just as good a lookout aft as you do for'ard – or be it on your own head.'

'What about enemy surface raiders?'

'I've never heard of one troubling a trawler.'

'Suppose we did see one of their battleships?'

'Funny, someone asked that question of Mr Sibley once. Know what the good man said? He said, "we'd signal the news to my Lords of Admiralty and go in with battle flag flying." '

'You're joking.'

'Don't take my word for it, dear boy – ask the worthy officer himself.'

Price was silent. James, languid at the wheel, lit another cigarette and blew some smoke.

'The truth of the matter is,' he said, 'the Northern Patrol was really devised to drive Ernie Michael dotty with the Asdic "pinging" in his one ear and Cross-Buckets "pinging" in the other. You ask Ernie – *he'll* tell you. Now what about that kye?'

When Price had served up cocoa all round and returned to his place as stand-by, James looked at him, smiling.

'I sense another question,' he said. 'Come on, out with it.'

'Why aren't you in for a commission course?'

'All the world's a stage, Pricey, and I know the part I want to play.'

'That's no answer.'

'It's mine, dear boy. It's mine. And it's all you're going to get.'

Young Brewster was taken ill in the middle of the night with stomach pains, so badly that Sub-Lieutenant Grant, who included 'medical officer' among his several roles, had to be sent for. After probing here and there he decided it couldn't be appendicitis and just gave the boy some pills.

'Price,' said William Campbell the Buffer, 'you're to be messman while yon laddie's sick.'

Price soon ceased to wonder at Brewster's initial queasiness and sudden illness. He found that the messman's job, besides its overpowering smell of food and slops, could be sheer misery to a novice; in a lurching, rolling ship it was a task which required speed, skill and efficiency while being cursed by the crew and screamed at by the harassed cook – 'If you canna get on top of this job I'll have to report you to Jimmy!' was his constant threat. His name was Towson, and he had cooked in fishing vessels pre-war and was appalled at the helplessness of the 'bloody civilians' with which the Navy was now filling the trawlers. He accompanied his terse instructions with sweeping gestures with whatever happened to be in his hand at the time, which was generally something sharp and lethal and to be avoided at all costs on a ship in full motion.

Midday dinner, the meal of the day, was by far the worst ordeal. It involved getting all the pots, pans, dishes and trays down from the galley, serving out the portions for each man – and they had better be equal! – passing all the food up to the galley again to be kept hot for the next sitting, grabbing the plates back from the dozen or so diners, washing them in a bucket, drying them and serving out the 'afters' on them, passing the 'afters' up to the galley again, grabbing the plates once more and washing them again in the bucket. Then the whole procedure had to be gone through all over again for the second sitting. Doing all this in a small pantry in a heavy sea made the sweat roll.

The weather was rough, and almost as soon as Price got down to his task the thick, steamy smell of food and hot tins made his head swim. He made four journeys up on deck to be sick during the morning, and by dinner-time hardly knew whether he was coming or going. Fiery language at his clumsy efforts flew at him from all directions, and he was feeling at his last gasp when suddenly big Ginger Meeson, who had been sitting grinning delightedly at the growing chaos, hoisted his huge bulk up from the table and, assisted by the sympathetic Wally Winters, took immediate efficient charge of the whole operation.

Price leaned against the bulkhead, sweat pouring down his face, and gratefully left things to the organising genius of the big man. On recovering he gritted his teeth, collected up plates and tins and carried on with the job, trying to close his nostrils against the more disgusting smells. After cleaning up following the last meal of the day, he had just enough energy left to struggle along for'ard, inevitably banging his head on the depth-charges, and turn in. But after that first bad spell he gradually got a hold of the job, his occasional mistakes and accidents, such as slipping wildly on the greasy deck and spilling the hot contents of the brimming tea 'fanny', amusing the crew rather than annoying them – 'Made another balls of it, Pricey?' However, he was far from sorry when, after two days, Brewster was pronounced well enough to resume his duties.

It was a relief to go back on watch, especially at night, when the sky was eerie with the Northern Lights. To see this strange ivory fire in the heavens, raying, peaking and fitfully flickering, was to sense the loneliness and desolation of the ice deserts of the far north whose reflection, some said, gave this light. He watched the show begin with a bar of light gleaming behind a cloud. Suddenly the light grew and streaked over the zenith to the west, a fiercely white arc-light. This was darkest night made day. The lights shot forth all over the sky, making strange convolutions, lively and mobile as mercury, branching off and rejoining the parent arc which was outdone by its offspring and made dull. The sea glimmered slate-grey, and the lights above became streaked with green and purple, very delicate and very beautiful.

Sub-Lieutenant Grant, the O.O.W., was in a talkative, helpful mood again.

'Price, what is your signalling form up to date?'

'Well, sir, I've swotted up the Naval flags, the international code, and I'm O.K. at semaphore – I can read the lamp if it's done slowly enough, but I don't get the chance for much practice.'

'No,' said Grant thoughtfully. 'Perhaps if I ask Bunts to spare you some time for lamp practice, that would help?'

Price thought rapidly. The notion of Grant ordering the signalman to give a C.W. man tuition was fraught with danger – the blasts from Signalman Garrett would reverberate through out the ship. He decided on the quick lie.

'Oh, he does give me some help, sir – thanks.'

'Really?'

Grant, who could only maintain a very tenuous relationship with his temperamental and much older signalman, covered his surprise with an approving nod.

'You say you know your Naval flags. Tell me what these flags are – affirmative, negative, letters H, K and P.'

'Affirmative – square red with white St George's Cross. Negative – white square with five black small crosses. H – square yellow with black circle in centre . . . K – square divided horizontally with yellow at top and blue on bottom . . . P – triangular all red.'

'Very good.' Grant studied his man. 'Price,' he said confidentially, 'you know that as a commission candidate you will be at a disadvantage coming from the Patrol Service. I was lucky, going to King Alfred training college from a destroyer, where they had a bunch of C.W.s together and had instruction classes – when there was time, which wasn't too often. Cruiser men are the luckiest, in those ships there *is* lots of time for instruction and lectures. An awful lot is going to depend on yourself and how much you can pick up along the way. And don't forget Officer-Like-Qualities – OLQ – very important at King Alfred. No one seems to know exactly what it means, but when you get there you must watch how you eat, how you walk, how you speak, how you play games, how you behave in and out of work time, how you address officers, how you sit in class. If they don't think you've got OLQ, then you're out.'

He paused diffidently.

'Don't hesitate to ask me any questions.'

'Thank you very much, sir.'

The subbie nodded and returned to the bridge-house.

During the night hours the *Emma*'s aft lookout divided his time, unofficially, between his post and the warm galley, the latter generally winning on balance. While at his post he would lean against or hug the funnel for warmth. Price, after his stint for'ard, took up his position aft and leaned against the warm, friendly funnel, watching, alternately, the sky and the sea until he had drifted off into a dreamy state of half wakefulness. Then James's story of the unfortunate *Derryman* came back to him and he screwed up his eyes to probe the dark sea receding behind them, though still reclining at ease. On hearing a sudden footfall he started up guiltily and looked round.

'Price! Smarten up, man. I expect more of *you*!' Sub-Lieutenant Sibley's voice came almost with a sneer.

'Yes, sir.'

'Keep alert at *all* times. Men's lives depend on *you*. Remember that. When you – if you – take charge you will bear the *ultimate* responsibility.'

'Yes, sir.'

'As a C.W. candidate I expect *you* to set an example for the rest of the crew.'

'Yes, sir.'

'You must *smarten up*.'

'Yes, sir.'

As Sibley grunted and strode off, Price blessed the good fortune that had kept him on deck instead of nipping down to the galley for a crafty warm.

By morning the sea had lost much of its strength and was almost idle in its rolling, trailing from its head nuptial veiling of delicate tracery like finely laundered lace. The hated order came from Sub-Lieutenant Sibley: more holystoning.

Those who were so inclined took opportunity in the fine weather to wash and shave. One of the first to do this was the sorrowful McDougal, who had once again suffered the lash of Sibley's tongue.

'Hear ye, hear ye,' said James, 'the Doog is washing his neck. Beware, the weather will take a turn for the worse.'

'Get stuffed.'

'My man, were I to take your instructions to heart, my entire innards would be of straw.'

McDougal was not alone in his vital ablutions. Stubby growth and grime were safely removed, the dirt coming off many necks like crude oil.

Smoke was seen at a distance and the *Lady Emma* set full speed towards it. It proved to be a sister trawler but, as the *Emma* drew nearer, a greater shape loomed up, three-funnelled and very large. Undaunted the little *Lady Emma* made towards her with gun-crews at their stations, and the big vessel resigned her dignity and hove to, to be duly challenged and give satisfaction.

'Why, I know that ship!' Price exclaimed. 'That's the *Carona* – the ship we went in on our Mediterranean cruise.'

Chief Hook, who had emerged from the bowels of the *Emma* to see what was going on, stared at him with fish-like, sceptical eye, grinned round sardonically at the others and growled,

'You're a rum booger, you are. Mediterranean cruise my Aunt Fanny – ha, ha, ha!'

Willie the Buffer, who was equally unconvinced, shook his head and murmured, 'Och, Price, but you're a terrible mon – a terrible mon!'

Eric Brewster edged in. 'Don't take any notice of them, Peter. She's a fine ship. I bet you had a real good time.'

But Price did not reply. He was remembering the sunny Mediterranean voyage and his father's boyish enthusiasm throughout it. His father, hearty and strong. Not blind and dying . . . and dead.

Just before nightfall a raft was sighted to starboard, but unfortunately lost again. Fearing that it might bear a survivor, the *Lady Emma* searched all through the night, her passage bringing her ever closer to Iceland. The dawn came up a glorious pink and purple, but still the sea was empty of anything but themselves and as they steamed nearer to the land the wind became increasingly cold. Even at two hours' steaming distance, great clarity of atmosphere made the island pleasant to view and to explore with the eye. The foothills, cliffs and crevices were a dark, volcanic black-brown, very sharp in outline against the sun-dazzling snow. They steamed nearer until they could see the surf quite plainly, and the rock-strewn glacier edges. A large merchant ship was aground, penned about with ice, but a brisk bout of signalling established that she was in no immediate danger and that help was on the way from the shore.

Farther inland they could see blockhouses, the significance of which was explained for Price's benefit by Wally Winters.

'They're set up about five miles apart all round the island – and Iceland's a good thousand miles in circumference, give or take a mile or two. They've all got food, clothes and cigarettes for any crews that are shipwrecked, and they've got a telephone link with Reykjavik and other towns.'

Winters went on to tell of his pal Bill Hewitt, who was a member of a crew wrecked off this same coast and who had spent a whole night walking barefoot through the snow in only his vest. After some hours the survivors stumbled on one of Iceland's volcanic springs and plunged themselves in it for warmth. The blockhouse they were aiming for was eventually reached, but, said Winters, they were very reluctant to leave that hospitable spring.

The *Emma* turned away from Iceland to follow her return line of patrol. The weather and sea roughened.

On night watch, Price went to relieve James on for'ard look-out and found him playing buses on the bridge verandah.

'Hurry along there, please, come along now . . . Plenty of lovely seats on top . . . Whoops, steady ducks . . . Right, up you go . . . Hurry along, guv, we haven't got all night . . . Hold tight please!' And he walked busily to and fro, taking money and tinging tickets.

'Warms me up,' he explained on seeing the arrival of his relief. 'And suppose I don't get into R.A.D.A., old boy? I'll have to do *something* for a living.'

Before leaving, after passing over his post, James gazed out at the night and became gloomily confidential.

'You know, Peter Price,' he said, 'I sometimes get the feeling that we'll never leave this spooky ship. None of us. We'll just go on sailing her for ever, back and forth, back and forth.'

'Like the Flying Dutchman?'

'That's right – like the Flying Dutchman. A phantom trawler searching for phantom U-boats, doomed to sail these forsaken northern seas for all eternity.'

'With occasional visits to the "Albert"?'

'Yes, Pricey old boy,' James smiled, coming slowly out of his reverie. 'With ghostly teas at the "Albert". Cheerio, see you back at the ranch.'

After his watch, during which he twice fell foul of Sub-Lieutenant Sibley, the O.O.W., and was crisply lectured for minor errors – 'You really must try harder, Price, *harder*' – he went below to thaw himself out over the glowing messdeck fire. Here, when a gale raged outside and the ship reeled, creaked and shuddered as she crashed down on each wave, they could sit snugly by that roaring blaze, stare deeply into the red-hot coals and imagine themselves back at home on a winter's night. It was an escapist paradise. The debates they had around that fire were legion. No topic of conversation was barred, and in the glow a man could expand and put forth his innermost thoughts to his shipmates.

As Price settled himself down, Ted Beckles was speaking. Beckles, like Eddie Nash, was a Londoner from the river, but years older than Eddie. Short of stature, sturdy and chubby with clear blue eyes, he would talk of the struggle between capitalism and the worker for hours – and he had a passionate dislike of foreigners. He was a truant from the Army, having come out of the hell of the beaches of Dunkirk and been sickened by the experience. But, being a true patriot, he had promptly volunteered for the Navy and the far-flung Patrol Service, and now lived in the hope that he would not be found out, for the water was his first love.

'I tell you it's all going to be different after the war,' he said over his pipe.

'How do you mean, Ted – different?'

'Well, all kinds of blokes mixed up together. Like us. Northerners, Southerners, Scots, Scouses, Yorkies, Welshies, posh blokes and real workers. All mixed up together, getting on together because we've got to. Bound to do away with a lot of class distinction after the war.'

'Come off it, Ted. It'll all go back to what it was as soon as everyone gets back into civvies.'

'No, it won't,' Beckles protested, 'it's been too much of a shake-up for that.'

'You can't change human nature, Ted – bosses will go back to being bosses again, and workers to being workers.'

'And McBride will go back to his Channel packet, ferrying the trippers across to France.'

'And Jimmy the One will get into films, like Robert Donat.'

'And Mr Sibley – he'll just go on being a bastard.'

'I'm serious, mates,' Beckles persisted. 'Folks will behave better to each other, they'll have more understanding.'

Geordie gave a huge snort.

'Don't you fool yourself. The Government won't care a monkey's toss when it's over. It'll be "Get back where you belong, you slobs" and there'll be a kick up the arse for anyone who don't jump to it.'

Wally Winters said with mock seriousness, 'I'm told, Geordie – on good authority – that they're going to make you Pit Manager when you get out of the Andrew.'

'Get stuffed, Winters. Our Maggie's a better liar than thee.'

'What happened after the last war, lads?' said Sam the fisherman. ' "A land fit for heroes to live in", they said, and soon there were millions of unemployed. How many men joined up this time from the dole?'

'That war was different,' said Beckles. 'It only touched the fighting men – it never touched the civvies, bar rationing and the odd bomb from a Zeppelin. This time they're all getting bombed. Must make it different, all being in it.'

'Aye, tha'll be a change in folks' thinking, tha knows, after his lot,' nodded Tiny taking a rare part in the discussion.

'An' let's 'ope it's a change for t'better,' said a fellow stoker. 'Ask thysen this – when danger's over, will folks forget all t'goodwill an' all?'

'They'll forget all right,' said Jack Barrow, a tattooed seaman who hailed from Liverpool. 'To get the good jobs you've got to wear the right kind of old school tie and belong to a golf club. All that won't change just because we've had another bloody war. They'll give you a few tin medals and a "Thank you very much' and send you back to the pit or the docks or the dole queue double quick.'

'Aw, what's the use of arguing about it?' said Eddie Nash. 'As long as I get out of this bleedin' mob and back to the Smoke, that's good enough for me. The sooner the better. And please Gawd, just let me bump into Cross-Buckets in the street . . . '

When the talk had subsided and the men had drifted away to their bunks James, who had been reading, walked lazily across and took a seat.

'The old Greek chorus is at it again, Pricey,' he said. 'What a lot of moaners we are, we are.' He poked the fire. 'I suppose you will be going back to the bank?'

'I haven't thought about it.'

'Back to your little window on the world. And Eric will go back to his Enid, and Ginger to his missus and six kids, and I'll be looking to carry a spear on stage somewhere . . . and all this will be just a bad dream. You know, Peter Price, the one certain thing is that all we'll become after the war is a lot of boring old men telling boring old tales, and the babies being born now won't want to know.'

Price wanted to contradict him, but could not. He remembered, with a twinge of shame, his own young disinterest in the annual parading of the 'Old Contemptibles' who had faced the armies of the Kaiser; and even in the experiences of his father, who had fought against the Turks.

James quoted,

' *"God and our sailors we adore,*
When danger threatens,
Not before.
With danger past,
Both are requited,
God forgotten, the sailor slighted."

'An old saying,' he added, 'from around 1740. Knew what he was on about, that shrewd fellow, didn't he?'

Suddenly the *Lady Emma* increased speed and one of the sea

60

men on watch scrambled down the messdeck ladder.

'There's a ship on fire, lads. We're going off to help her.'

Soon the Buffer was passing on orders and men were busy. A crew was detailed for the whaler. The *Emma*'s fire-fighting appliances were made ready and hoses connected to pressure points. Men got out the reserve of blankets for use when picking up survivors.

'How many crew has she?'

'About sixty, they say.'

'That's a big 'un.'

The *Emma*'s two stretchers were found and Sub-Lieutenant Grant laid out the first-aid equipment. The cook was told to prepare food and drinks, and extra messmen were detailed off.

The ship in trouble was sighted far away in the fitful moonlight, a thin stream of grey smoke on the horizon. Slowly her masts and funnel became visible, and as the *Emma* drew still nearer, with all hands on voluntary lookout, it was evident that the fire on board had grown in intensity. Like a naked torch flung on to the water the flames leapt skyward, turning night into day, while above the flames great palls of dense smoke billowed and spread out into the edges of darkness.

The whaler's crew sat in the boat with two men at the falls, ready to lower away. The *Emma* stopped engines.

'Lower away handsomely!' came the order, and gently and evenly the whaler, with Sub-Lieutenant Grant in charge, descended into the sea. The Buffer's voice was heard, 'Let go the falls – give way together!' An oar pushed the boat away from the trawler's side and the men began to row.

A lamp started flashing from the stricken ship and Signalman Garrett, on the *Emma*'s bridge, concentrated hard to get its message. The flashing was slow and amateurish, and the operator made a hash of it, wiped it out with a scatter of dots and then began again. Garrett called out the words as he read them.

'Do not . . . come close . . . we . . . are full . . . of . . . ammunition . . . '

Quickly seizing the loud-hailer McBride repeated the message to the whaler, adding, 'Mr Grant – keep rowing but do not, repeat not, go closer than half a mile from the ship and await my further orders.' He then went into urgent conference with Hadley and Sibley.

The situation was speedily known on deck.

'What the hell do we do now?' said Eddie Nash. 'We can't let those poor bastards fry.'

'They'll launch their own lifeboats,' said Sam reassuringly.

'Suppose the fire's burnt 'em?'

'They'll have rafts. Merchant ships carry dozens.'

'Well, why haven't they launched them, then?'

Jack Barrow spat. 'Their skipper doesn't want to lose his ship – hoping to put the bloody fire out, I'll wager.'

'I wouldn't put any money on that,' Sam murmured.

On the bridge Signalman Garrett was desperately trying to read another message from the burning ship, but the flickering, spurting flames now mingled with the flashing, making it a hopeless jumble.

'Send "How close to fire is explosive?" ' ordered McBride.

Garrett sent the message and repeated it, but could get no recognisable reply.

McBride fumed. 'Why has she stopped using her wireless? Signalman, keep sending that message.' He dared not take the *Lady Emma* closer in without having obtained more information from the merchantman. He spoke into the engineroom voicepipe, 'Chief, stand by.'

The whaler, having reached its ordered distance, sat motionless on the water, its crew silent as they watched and waited. The flames licked ever upwards and were reflected in a calm sea which framed the scene in a ruddy glow.

'See anything, sir?'

'No.' Sub-Lieutenant Grant was looking for a boat, a raft, any sign of men abandoning ship, but there was nothing. Once or twice he thought he saw figures moving on the merchantman's deck, but he could not be sure.

On the bridge of the *Emma* McBride made his decision.

'Slow-ahead.'

Eric Brewster, who was watching on deck with Price, pointed excitedly.

'Look – I think the fire's going down – they must be getting it under control.'

Hardly had he spoken the last word when ship, flames, smoke, everything was obliterated by an enormous orange flash, followed almost immediately by a tremendous bang which left the ears singing; and then came a blast of hot air which flung men to the *Emma*'s deck and rocked the horrified crew of the whaler. Out of the great orange ball of fire there shot a mass of debris – bits and pieces of it being recognisable as part of a bridge, a mast, a boiler, a gun-barrel, half a lifeboat, sacks, boxes, huge pieces of timber and metal, and – unmistakable in the blinding glare – a few tiny human figures which kicked and twisted in the air like marionettes. For a few brief moments this ghastly tableau seemed to stand still and frozen, and then, as in a slow-motion film, to sink back into the sea. The glare subsided, the great smoke pall rose upwards – and there was nothing.

On board the *Lady Emma* there was a stunned silence, broken at last by a hoarse voice.

'Them poor bastards!'

The whaler returned, the trawler's engines started up, and with scrambling nets ready she steamed slowly to circle the spot where there had lately been a handsome ship. As dawn broke they spotted debris floating in the sea, but no survivors and not even a body.

A hooting, threshing corvette arrived to continue the search and the *Emma* was summarily instructed to return to her patrol.

'Sixty men,' said Wally Winters. 'Where have they gone?'

7

Through sheeting rain the *Lady Emma* passed the Butt of Lewis, northernmost point of the Hebrides, and it was still pelting down relentlessly as she turned Cape Wrath and began the final run to the Orkneys. She arrived at Kirkwall in a watery dawn.

Signalman Garrett came down from the bridge and ruefully faced the many pairs of questioning eyes.

'Sorry, lads. It's a hundred and sixty tons.'

Somehow they had all guessed the worst, but that did not lessen the blow nor stifle the groans.

'Bastards!'

'It's those shore-bound clerks – they've buggered it up again. It *must* be our turn for refit.'

'We'll *never* get home.'

'Why doesn't the Old Man do something about it? That's what I want to know.'

Jerry the steward silently began to unpack his suitcases yet again.

They spent a miserable day coaling up in the persistent drizzle, a tedious, wet and dirty job not enlivened even by the fact that Lieutenant Hadley was actually seen to use a shovel for ten minutes before finding other, more pressing business. But at least afterwards there was the mail. The letters and parcels distributed, they were swapping bits of domestic news and big Ginger, having read his single message from home, was singing 'Pennies From Heaven' out of tune, fondly imagining himself to sound like Bing Crosby, when Eddie Nash, who had been on deck talking to the men on the visiting storeboat, came down the messdeck ladder grim of face and stood looking at the group seated round the blazing fire.

'What's the matter, Eddie?'

'The *Ocean Crystal*'s gone.'

'So what?'

'She's gone to Iceland – to be a convoy escort.'

'Coastal convoys? Well, anything's better than the Northern Patrol.'

'No, not coastal convoys,' said Nash agitatedly. 'They say she's going on convoy to Russia!'

'What, the old *Crystal*? Up in the Arctic? They must be stark raving bloody mad!' said Tommy Tilson.

'She's a hundred tons bigger than us,' said Wally Winters, 'and better built. They'll be all right.'

'I'm not worried about the bleedin' *Crystal*, mate. The buzz is that other trawlers are going to be sent on the Russian run.'

The silence that followed was broken by a hearty laugh from Jack Barrow.

'You mean, they might send the *Emma*? Up in that ice? Not on your bloody life!'

Big Ginger broke into peals of laughter, and Eddie Nash's face reddened.

'They're crazy enough to send a bleedin' barge if they feel like it,' he argued.

'Don't worry, Eddie,' said Winters, 'we've got our hundred and sixty tons – we know where *we're* going. There's plenty of bigger trawlers around if they need them.'

'I still don't like it.'

'Sounds bloody daft to me,' said Barrow. 'It takes a trawler all its time to keep up with an ordinary convoy. What do they think the buggers can do up there?'

As Barrow threw out a challenging tattooed arm in the direction of the northern wastes, Price tried to picture the route a convoy to Russia would take, but failed. Those remote seas, he remembered, had looked cold and inhospitable enough on a map – the very edge of the world. What it would be like in reality he could not imagine. He gave an involuntary shiver.

'If they're short of escorts they'll make 'em go just the same,' said a voice gloomily.

'Better them than us.'

'A lot of trawlers were built for those seas,' said Winters. 'Even the *Emma*'s been out near Bear Island.'

'Maybe – *fishing*. But she's no bloody ice-breaker – none of 'em are. And the winter ice is thick and treacherous.'

'It's a job for corvettes and destroyers – real warships, not these slow old boats.'

'That's true, but if it comes to the push they'll take anything that floats. You see.'

'Not the *Emma* they bloody won't! Next time we *are* due for G.Y. and refit.'

'Good luck to the *Crystal*, poor buggers. You've been in those freezing seas, Wally – are they really bad?'

Winters gazed thoughtfully into the fire.

'It's about as cold as a man can get,' he said. 'You go over-board in the Arctic and you'll be lucky to last five minutes.'

'That's bloody cheerful!'

'I've heard tell of men who were only in the water for half that time and still had to lose a limb.'

'Aw, get knotted,' said Eddie Nash.

Big Ginger broke into more peals of laughter. Tommy Tilson savagely stirred the fire, causing a burst of flames. 'They'll never get *me* up among those soddin' Eskimos,' he said belliger-ently. 'I've put in for the Fleet Air Arm.'

'Hey, lads, now Tommy's going to fly!'

'You have your fun. But when I'm an aircraft fitter on one of those big carriers and I think of you lot rattling about in this old rat-trap, I'll do the laughing. Aye, aye, sir, three bags full – I'll laugh my bloody head off.'

'You won't if we go to Canada, chum.'

They had heard earlier of some trawlers crossing the Atlantic to help out the Royal Canadian Navy.

'Those were Admiralty-built trawlers.'

'Not all of 'em, there were requisitioned boats too.'

'Just fancy us taking James back home to Canada!'

'We could even go down to the States.'

The sudden thought of plenty of silk stockings and other booty for wives and girl friends fired every mind. There had been a 'buzz' that some trawlers had gone off to the Florida coast to work with the Americans against the U-boats; that would be money for old rope.

'Aw, some hopes,' said Eddie Nash. 'Can you imagine the *Emma* out in the middle of the Atlantic? The bleedin' funnel would fall off!'

'Pipe dreams,' sighed Ted Beckles, puffing away at his briar.

The thoughts of silk stockings and all else faded fast as they came back to raw reality.

Eric Brewster was in his bunk savouring newly received letters from home. 'Peter,' he said delightedly, 'I'm going into business with Enid's dad. It's all settled and we're going to fix it up properly when I get leave.'

'What kind of business?'

'A garage, of course. You know how I've always messed about with motor-cycles, well, Mr Stapleton's going to teach me car mechanics – he's pretty expert – and we'll start up together. There's a big future in cars, you know. One day everybody will have one, not just the well-off.'

'Could be.'

'What did you say your car was?'

'An MG Midget.'

'Yes – *that's* the kind of car I'd like to take to pieces and put back together again.'

'Not mine you won't.'

Brewster laughed happily.

'Have you ever had it to pieces?'

'No. As long as she goes, that's good enough for me.'

'What's it like being in a bank?'

'Dull. Very dull.'

'You know, Peter, I can't wait to get married.'

'Then don't wait.'

'That's what Enid says.'

'She's a sensible girl.'

'Yes, but – ' Brewster frowned. 'I mean, you never know what's going to happen . . . how long this war is going to last.'

'You get married and I'll come to the wedding.'

'You would? You really would?'

Price looked at the boy's earnest face.

'Yes, I'll come. I promise.'

Next day Brewster to his disappointment was earmarked for Quartermaster, which kept him on board while the first batch of libertymen went ashore. He filled in his time beforehand having a good wash-up of all his clothes, and to everyone's great surprise obtained permission from Chief Hook to hang some up to dry in the engineroom, a rare privilege for a seaman.

'Don't tell me that suspicious-minded man is becoming human,' said James. 'Beware of chief enginemen bestowing favours.'

'He's good-hearted under it all,' said Brewster, grinning.

'Real fatherly, eh? I'd rather trust old Neptune himself.'

Soon Brewster had finished washing a vast assortment of

garments which he hung all over the ship, in the engineroom and at the messdeck fire, and went round inspecting his handiwork with the fine glow of achievement.

'Have it all nicely ironed when we get back,' said James, and ducked to avoid a swipe with a wet seaboot stocking.

The rain had stopped, but a biting wind whistled through the rugged town of Kirkwall, bringing with it swirls of sleet. However, it could not mar the pleasure of having solid earth under one's feet instead of a pitching deck, and there were more pleasures to come.

'Come on, Pricey,' said James. 'Step lively!'

'Where are we going?'

'For a bath, dear boy. Oh, joy!'

He led Price at a brisk pace to a large, many-chimneyed house on the outskirts of the town.

'It's a kind of hostel,' he said as they walked up the drive, 'run by some very charming ladies. I've stayed here a few times on an overnight pass. They'll allow us a bath – let me do the talking.'

He rang the bell and after a short wait the heavy door opened.

'Hello, Sister Ann.'

James beamed as he removed his cap and thumped Price in the middle of his back to do the same. The nun gave a smile of recognition and bade them enter.

James explained regretfully that they had not got overnight passes but they had just returned from patrol and could they please, please have a bath? The nun went off to consult someone unseen and returned again smiling.

'Yes, Mr Crawford, and your friend. Certainly you may. Please follow me.'

The nun held her rosary beads with one small, birdlike hand as she took them up the stairs of the quiet house. From a cupboard she produced a large white towel for each of them, together with a tablet of soap.

'Thank you, Sister.'

The nun inclined her head, then indicated the two bathrooms, one at each end of the corridor, and withdrew noiselessly down another passage with only a hint of black shoes moving beneath her voluminous black gown.

'Okay,' said James. 'Off we go. Only one thing – no singing.'

They were in their respective bathrooms in no time and running the sparkling clear water. Stepping into the spotless, steaming bath, lolling back into the hot water, soaping himself from head to toe, seeing the dirt of two weeks' living rough on board ship rolling off his body, a glorious relaxation swept over Price like a tidal wave and he lay there for a time in a state of euphoria.

When they were dressed again and ready to leave, James dashed off to thank the nun. When he reappeared, Price asked, 'How do we pay them?'

'Oh, have it on me, old boy,' said James grandly. He dropped some coins into a box beside a statuette of the Holy Virgin, and quietly they let themselves out.

Later they paused in front of Kirkwall Cathedral, feeling glowing and clean under their uniforms.

'This little pile is dedicated to St Ola, the first Christian missionary to these islands, way back in A.D. 45,' said James. 'A trifle before the Patrol Service discovered them. I feel I should have known Mr Ola, we've been coming back here so often.'

The doors of the cathedral were dulled with rain and sun, the studs and hinges rusty.

'Did you know King Arthur was of Orkney stock? Oh well, never mind . . .'

They joined the queue for the 'Albert' and disposed of a lavish tea, enjoying once more a breath of home in the tearoom's cleanliness and goodwill.

'Soon,' said James, licking the last spot of quince jam from his lips, 'we'll have the greatest pleasure of all. On leave, sleeping in pyjamas instead of crawling into kip fully dressed.'

'You think the *Emma* will definitely go for refit after our next patrol?'

'Bound to.'

'Well, at least that means we won't be going to Russia.'

'Meaning you'll get to training college so much sooner?' James looked at him with amusement in his eyes. 'Peter Price,' he said, 'you are always asking the questions. Now let me ask you one. What makes you want to be an officer?'

'Because I think I can do it.'

'Run a ship?'

'Yes.'

'Make decisions?'

'Yes.'

'Control men who have been at sea all their lives while you were at school or scribbling in bank ledgers?'

'Yes.'

James was thoughtful.

'In the trawlers,' he said, 'most men have been going to sea since they left school, and the skippers and mates all came up from the ranks. What these deep sea fishermen can't understand is how a pen-pusher can do half a dozen weeks' training ashore, go to sea for three months, then go off on a quick course and emerge as an officer, while they themselves, with years of sea-going experience, are not considered "officer material". To their minds it doesn't make sense – but you know that, don't you.'

'Yes.'

'Put yourself in their place. How would you like to be down on the messdeck in a full gale, knowing that you were up there in charge of the ship?'

'I still think I could do it.'

'Then good luck to you, and don't let our Mr Sibley put a spoke in your wheel. Have a Player.'

They lit up, and James blew smoke rings.

'When you are driving your destroyer,' he said, 'spare a thought for your old mates. Better still, when it's all over, tell our side of it. Write a book about us. Never mind the Admirals and their view from the jolly old bridge, you give it to the customer straight.'

'A boring book by a boring old man?'

'Tell the humble *Emma*'s story. Make her famous. You never know, two or three people might be interested in how *we* went to war.'

'Why me?'

'Well, you're the pen-pusher, dear boy. You have a literary reputation – didn't you know? Haven't you seen the way big Ginger looks at you?'

'I try to keep a diary, that's all. If anyone does any writing it should be you.'

'Me? I'm merely a strolling player. Fancy free, me and my old Mum back in Toronto. How's your Mum?'

'She died when I was eight years old.'

'Oh. I'm sorry. So you're alone now?'

'I have a sister. She's married.'

'Well, it shouldn't be too long before she sees you in officer's rig. Do you like gin?'

'No.'

'Then you'll have to acquire a taste for it. Come on, time for the flicks and Mickey Rooney, and the newsreel telling us what brave sons of the sea we all are.'

'As they were leaving, James turned for a last look at the inside of the 'Albert'. 'I wonder,' he said, 'when we'll be back to this joyous house again . . . ?'

After the cinema they had just time to grab fish and chips before catching the drifter and shivering throughout the journey back to the *Lady Emma*, anchored this time at the entrance to the harbour.

'Price!'

It was mid-afternoon the following day and he was idling on deck practising sending a morse message with an invisible Aldis lamp. The beginner's trick in operating the Aldis, Bob Garrett had told him, as you never saw the flashes you were sending, was to make a noise like the trigger of the lamp as it clicked back and forward again – an 'iddy' for a dot, and a longer 'umpty' for a dash. When interrupted he was sending the name of the ship – 'iddy umpty iddy iddy . . . iddy umpty . . . umpty iddy iddy . . . umpty iddy umpty umpty . . . iddy . . . '

'Yes, sir?'

'Smarten up, man,' said Sub-Lieutenant Sibley. 'Tell Michael to report to me in the Wardroom.'

'Aye, aye, sir.'

He went down to the P.O's mess, took off his cap and opened the door. Ernie Michael had his feet up, reading a newspaper.

'Mr Sibley wants – ' he began.

'I *know* what that bastard wants!' snarled the Higher Submarine Detector, snatching up a seaboot from the floor and aiming it.

Price swiftly shut the door and got as far away as possible. He found Willie the Buffer, with his spectacles perched on his nose, checking through store lists. At such times the gentle Scot looked like an owlish parson dressed up as a sailor.

'Are ye settling down, Price? Mr Grant speaks well of ye.'

'Yes, thanks. Can I help you with the checking?'

'No thank ye, son. I have to do it in my own way. Will ye be restowing the emergency blankets now?'

As he performed this task Price could not help remembering the vivid scene as the ammunition ship blew up, and he was thoroughly glad when the job was done. He hated himself for his roving imagination. Was that an 'Officer-Like-Quality'?

During the evening he narrowly escaped falling foul of Sibley and Ernie Michael, deep in a heated exchange on the after deck.

'It's a load of balls!'

'Michael, I warn you – '

'Who has to work the bloody thing – you or me?' growled the H.S.D. 'Who has charge of the equipment? Who has to do the running repairs?'

'Mr Hadley says . . . '

'Mr Hadley can go and take a running jump. What does he know?'

'The Asdic instructions clearly lay down – '

'All right, *Mister* Sibley, you take over and do it your bloody way.'

'I will not tolerate such insolence, and furthermore – '

'My arse,' said Michael.

'Report to the C.O. at once!'

'And what do I tell him when I get there?'

Price crept away and out of earshot.

When the libertymen returned, Jack Barrow was first with the news.

'The *Jessie Logan*'s sailed for Iceland. She's off to Russia like the *Crystal*.'

'There – what did I bleedin' well tell you?' said Eddie Nash.

'The *Jessie*'s bigger than us – they're after the big ones all right,' said Wally Winters.

'We'll finish up being the only buggers on patrol.'

'That'll put the fear of Christ up Jerry!'

Brewster returned carrying a large brown paper parcel.

'I've bought myself a suit,' he said happily, and dug out a blue West of England jacket and trousers.

'Put it on then, lad!'

'Really? Oh, all right.'

When it was on he began walking about, self-consciously at first and then with growing confidence.

'What do you think?'

'Smashing.'

'A good bit of cloth there, boy.'

'But doesn't your girl prefer to see you in uniform?'

'No,' Brewster took off the jacket and carefully smoothed out some imaginary creases. 'It worries her. Not all the time, but, well . . . '

'It's a good suit, laddie.'

'Ought to be. It cost me sixteen bob.'

'Worth every penny,' said Price. It really was a good fit.

Brewster took off the trousers and folded them, then relaxed on his bunk and thought dreamily of meeting Enid in his suit.

Ginger was singing, wildly off key, 'I wouldn't leave my little

72

wooden hut for you . . . ' He had refused all invitations to play cards, being content to rest after his evening's drinking. Last back on board was Paddy Kelly. A set smile on his face, he came slowly down the messdeck ladder as if intent on not spilling a drop.

'How are you, Mr Price?'

'I'm fine, Mr Kelly.'

'That's me bhoy!'

In five minutes the big Irishman had collapsed on his bench in front of the fire and had to be carried off to his bunk.

James came down after finishing his stint as Quartermaster and, gathering together a book and all kinds of odds and ends, got into his hammock, flopping V-shaped with his bottom an inch or two off the deck. Catching Price's eye he grinned and whipped off a smart salute.

Brewster had a sudden idea and looked down from his top bunk.

'I'll change into the suit in the lavatory on the train – that'll surprise her at the station. What do you think, Peter?'

'A splendid idea.'

The *Lady Emma* was due to sail at noon and the Buffer had given the crew their working orders.

'Price, Barrow, your leaving harbour station is the chain-locker.'

'That bloody lousy rat-hole!' said Jack Barrow.

'Now then, Barrow, ye know the ropes and can explain things to your partner.'

Barrow glowered at the Buffer, then at Price, and walked away in disgust.

Big Ginger moved over to Price and stared down at him gravely.

'So you're going to be our new Chain-Locker Charlie, eh? It's a proper mucky job – you'll stink like buggery for a week afterwards. Can't get the stuff off you. Dangerous, too. You get your hands caught in that bloody anchor cable and your own mother wouldn't recognise you. I knew a bloke who did just that, and it took us half an hour to scrape the mess of him off the cable. We put it all into buckets and chucked it over the side. So watch it, lad!'

When the preparations for leaving harbour began, Price followed Barrow along the deck for'ard until they came to a trapdoor which Barrow opened, and they climbed down a ladder into a stiflingly small compartment which reeked of the worst dank ocean smells. The slimy anchor chain or 'cable' hung taut from the hawsepipe, falling away into heavy coils at the bottom of the locker, and there was a tiny platform each side of it on which they took up their positions, wearing heavy gloves. The headroom was such that they could not stand upright, and they crouched and waited for the trawler to lift her anchor.

'What's the drill then, Jack?'

'Just guide the cable down so that it coils up evenly on the bottom. If you don't watch it the bastard gets jammed in the pipe if the links pile up one on top of the other. Got it?'

They heard the winch being run on the foc's'le above and the order, 'Prepare to heave in!' Then, down the hawsepipe, 'Are you all ready down there?'

'Aye bloody aye!'

'Then heave away.'

The winch rumbled, there was a loud clanking noise and the great cable began to descend slowly from the hawsepipe. Price and Barrow leaned forward and grasped and guided the slimy links to fall into even coils at the bottom of the pit. It was heavy work and Barrow kept up a flow of curses. The pace increased and their arms ached to keep up with the swinging cable. Barrow yelled up the pipe, 'Not so fast, you silly buggers! Slow it down or I'll bloody well quit.'

His threat fell on deaf ears and suddenly he moved back and shouted, 'All right, we'll show 'em – let go, Pricey, let it jam!'

Left on his own now Price fought desperately to control the snaking, clanking links and guide them into their coils, but it was too heavy a task for one inexperienced man and as the links piled up into an untidy and mounting heap the inevitable happened and the cable jammed under the pipe.

The winch stopped and a voice bellowed, 'What's happened below?'

Barrow retorted angrily, 'It's bloody jammed – you're heaving in too fast for us! Slow it a bit.'

'Nonsense, Barrow,' snapped back the voice of Sub-Lieutenant Sibley. 'You are not doing your job properly! Smarten up, both of you – and stand well clear, I'm going to veer to clear the jam.'

They leaned right back and it was well that they did, for with a terrifying jerk the links suddenly untangled, shot out in all directions and then up the pipe until the winch-brake was applied. Then, 'Stand by to heave again!' and clank, clank, clank, down came the cable once more and this time Barrow, with a new flow of running curses, did his part, the coils settled down neatly, the winch-brake was applied, the cable-stops secured, and the great cable was still. Two slime-coated, stinking figures emerged from the chain-locker trapdoor and the *Lady Emma* was under way, bound for the open sea.

Men moved discreetly out of the way of the 'Chain-Locker Charlies'. James demonstratively held his fingers to his nose, while big Ginger gusted with laughter.

Price felt and smelt as though he had been dragged through a sewer. Even the bitingly fresh sea air did little to dissipate the stench that hung about him.

Ah well, there was the memory of that bath . . .

8

On the fourth day of the *Lady Emma*'s patrol, with the evening light fading on a settled sea, the watch-below was roused to action by the shrill clamour of the alarm-bells –

'Submarine alert!'

Every man sped to his action-station, the four-inch gun crew having good reason to curse Sub-Lieutenant Sibley for his diligence in ordering the steps leading to the gun platform to be painted only hours before. The paint came off messily on hands, boots and clothes. They stood-to, shivering.

'Mr Sibley, stand by depth-charges.'

'Aye, aye, sir. Meeson, Barrow, Nash, Beckles – stand by!'

On the bridge Ernie Michael had taken over from the jittery Swanson to monitor the ominous message of the Asdic as the pointer needle jerked and quivered.

Ping-ping . . . ping-ping . . . ping-ping . . .

The mysterious object was plotted as being only a mile and a half away. McBride conned the ship to the Asdic's bearings, setting her bows square on to the target.

'Full-ahead!'

Michael was calm, hunched in his chair at the Asdic control, checking the strength of echo, distance and bearing.

'Contact still firm, sir. Estimated depth eighty to ninety feet . . . on target.'

McBride gave orders through the loud-hailer. 'Set for one hundred feet.'

Sibley repeated the command, and the men with the keys set the depth-charges to be rolled off the rails aft and shot from the port throwers.

The tone of the Asdic altered.

'Losing contact, sir.'

'Impossible!'

'Lost contact, sir.'

'Find him, man!'

'Could it have been a shoal of fish?' asked Lieutenant Hadley drily.

'No, sir.' Michael highly resented the suggestion that he had been fooled by the common fluctuation of the Asdic on striking a body of fish or a wreck.

'How can you be sure?'

Michael ground his teeth before replying: 'I know a fish contact, sir.'

'A submarine could not just disappear.'

'No, sir.' Michael swore vehemently under his breath.

For an hour as twilight faded into night the *Lady Emma* kept up her search, but without result. Then a light flickered in the darkness. It was another trawler. She, too, reported a submarine contact and gave the position. McBride did some quick calculations and decided to join forces with the other vessel to 'find, attack and sink'.

Ernie Michael, mollified now that his skill as a Higher Submarine Detector had been vindicated, hung on to the searching sound beam of the Asdic like a bulldog on the tail of a coat. At last they made contact again. *Ping-ping . . . ping-ping . . .* He called out the bearing.

'Emergency full-ahead!'

At McBride's sharp command the *Emma* threshed towards the target, leaving her sister trawler still sweeping somewhere in the darkness.

'Prepare to fire depth-charges.'

'Aye, aye, sir.'

'Roll away!'

But at the critical moment the depth-charges stuck in their rails and the best the firing party could do was to trigger off a solitary 'can' from one of the throwers, the underwater explosion from which shook the ship like a leaf.

McBride's savage language rent the night. Under frenzied directions from Sibley the depth-charge party tried to ease the rail depth-charges free, ready for another attempt at rolling them off, but a new command from the bridge put an end to their struggles. The Asdic contact had been lost again and whatever it was below the surface of the night sea had now disappeared entirely. In minutes the other trawler loomed up, and there followed a quick-fire and very descriptive dialogue by Aldis lamp as both skippers gave vent to pent-up feelings.

'It's a good job we didn't drop a pattern,' said Eddie Nash, 'or we'd have gone down to join the bleedin' fish.'

They stood down from action-stations and the *Lady Emma* resumed her line of patrol.

Next morning, in a pitching sea, while McBride glowered down from the bridge, Sub-Lieutenant Sibley had the depth-charge party drilling, drilling, drilling at their stations till their arms and legs ached from their exertions. 'Guns', not to be outdone, put the gun-crew through their paces, and Price, during his labours, looked up to see James, on for'ard lookout, affect an empty sleeve and a blind eye as he mockingly struck a pose like Nelson sighting the enemy. The furious activity on deck only came to an end when the weather turned suddenly and the heavens opened, sending them scuttling for cover, half-drowned in spite of their oilskins.

'Never a dull moment,' said James breezily as Price, oozing water, relieved him on lookout. 'Here we all are, looking like the label on a tin of Skipper's sardines.'

The storm lasted till nightfall, ending a thoroughly dismal and angry day for everyone. Then, with the coming of a bleak but dry dawn, the routine of patrol began again, with more challenges filling the *Emma*'s log. The monotony of life on patrol reasserted itself and they began to wish the days away, the hours even. Conversation dried up and tempers became short. The symptoms were unmistakable: the one common thought was of refit.

On the afternoon of the seventh day a destroyer sped over the horizon and steamed importantly in a wide sweep around the trawler as if conducting a snap inspection.

'Bloody show-offs!' said Jack Barrow.

The destroyer, having amply sized up the *Lady Emma*, began a long conversation by lamp. On receiving the destroyer's final message McBride looked perplexed and disbelieving, and curtly requested it to be repeated. When the wording came over exactly as before, he boldly questioned the authority for the order it contained, and in reply was given confirmation in swift and forthright language by the annoyed destroyer captain.

McBride's face reddened as Signalman Garrett read out the message. For a minute he hesitated, then he snapped out commands.

As the *Lady Emma* performed a 180 degree turn, Eddie Nash bolted down from his stand-by position on watch to yell the news breathlessly to the messdeck.

'I knew it – I bleedin' *knew* it! They're off their rocker – we're turning back and heading for Iceland!'

They looked at him, appalled and speechless, all except James, who glanced up idly from his Shakespeare.

'Break out the snowshoes, lads. Harness the huskies.'

'Get stuffed.'

Big Ginger began to shake with laughter, but everyone else felt a certain sickness in their stomachs.

'It can't mean Russia, surely,' said Brewster, shaking his head. 'It just can't . . .'

Signalman Garrett came slowly down the messdeck ladder and they read in his tensed face the awful truth.

'It's right, lads,' he said. 'We've been ordered to rendezvous for convoy duty forthwith. We're finished with the Northern Patrol. We're bound for Reykjavik.'

'What about our refit?'

'What about our leave?'

'What about the bloody boilers?'

Garrett, ignoring the questions flung at him from all directions, sat down and put his head in his hands. He was thinking of his wife and newly born child.

'Yo ho, heave ho,' said James.

'Shut your bloody trap!' shouted Geordie.

'Now lads . . .' said Willie the Buffer.

Wally Winters threw more coal on to the messdeck fire. 'Well,' he commented, 'no more patrols for us. There's a lot of good in that.'

Even the weather now kept fine to speed them with indecent haste towards Iceland, and there was a brooding awareness that, this time, every mile they covered in that direction could be a point of no return.

The land, at first sight, might have been low lying cloud banks, but a second glance revealed a certain solidarity which in the course of time turned out to be orange hued mountains, pastel in the sunlight and as unreal in aspect as a Chinese scroll painting. This was a new face of Iceland, many miles distant.

It was turning colder by the minute and Price, on lookout, was chilled to the bone, too frozen even to take interest when the *Emma* passed a large school of whales, which appeared to be the only inhabitants of the rigorous waters. If it was as cold as this off the south of Iceland, what must it be like north of the Arctic Circle? His watch over, he fled gladly for the comfort of the messdeck fire.

Hour after hour the *Lady Emma* rode into the cold waters, steaming round the southern tip of Iceland and taking her crew farther west than they had ever been before, her engines beating out the miles to Reykjavik.

It was evening, and the watch-below was huddled round the messdeck fire when a chirpy voice shouted down the hatch.

'Come up on top, you lucky lads, and see the Blackpool illuminations! It's all lit up!'

And it was. Forgetting the cold, they leaned on the ship's rail, staring curiously at the first town with its lights up that they had seen since August 1939 – two and a half years ago. This was Reykjavik, the capital of Iceland, land of the sagas, home of the descendants of the ancient Vikings. Reykjavik – all lit up. Tiny cars with blazing headlights could be seen threading their way through the streets. The twinkling lights of the houses, emphasising their whiteness, went glittering away up the hill on which the town was built. They feasted their eyes on the spectacle of fairyland.

'It's like we've left the war behind,' said Jack Barrow incredulously. 'Haven't they heard of the blackout?'

'They don't need it out here.'

'The Americans have taken over now.'

'Might have known – just like the bloody Yanks. What do they think this is, Coney Island?'

'Can't imagine any Jerry bombers flying out here anyway. They'd run out of petrol.'

'Or bloody freeze to death.'

There were other ships and boats in the bay, lying dark and silent in contrast. The *Lady Emma* dropped anchor, and speculation ran high that they might get a run ashore next day.

The night grew colder still, wrapping the trawler in an icy cocoon. Everything froze, given the slightest chance. Both the capstan and the for'ard winch had to be kept turning slowly throughout the night to avoid being frozen solid. A cup of hot cocoa left on deck was turned into brown ice in an incredibly short space of time. The fresh-water pipes running the length of the ship froze up and next morning the stokers had to thaw them out by burning paraffin-soaked pieces of waste on them.

Hopes that they might taste the delights of Reykjavik were very soon dashed. New orders were received and the *Lady*

Emma sailed at noon. After two hours' steaming she reached the entrance to a fiord where a number of merchant ships were gathered awaiting convoy, along with some Naval escorts.

'It's called Hvalfiord,' Sparks told them. 'But you don't pronounce the "H".'

'Like bloody old Scapa I call it,' said Barrow. 'Only worse. What a Godforsaken hole!'

Hvalfiord was a very large and desolate stretch of water, like a Scottish loch, with a wide entrance protected by a long boom, outside which a big trawler steamed slowly back and forth on anti-submarine patrol. The boom was raised and lowered by two boom defence vessels. When the *Lady Emma* was through the boom her crew saw that the fiord was fully as bleak as it had seemed at first sight. The low, hilly land encompassing it was featureless and drab, the only sign of habitation ashore being a few Nissen huts dotted about at one point. The fiord ended miles inland, where the low hills rose steeply into snow-capped mountains. Under grey skies it all looked very grim.

'Twenty-two,' said Eddie Nash. He had been counting merchant ships. 'Nothing to write home about, are they? No big buggers.'

'There's the *Flora Russell*,' said Wally Winters, pointing to a trawler anchored among the few Naval escorts. 'She's a fine Aberdeen boat. I had a trip in her once.'

'What are they doing with minesweepers?' said Ted Beckles. 'Look, there's two of them next to that sloop.'

'I don't suppose they do any sweeping,' said Barrow. 'They've enough fire-power to make good escorts. See those guns?'

Tommy Tilson hung over the rail.

'Sweepers,' he said gloomily. 'I thought of volunteering for them once, but sweeping for mines day after day would drive me into the bloody nuthouse.'

After a short wait the *Lady Emma* steamed towards the Base ship for Naval escort vessels, a huge, coal-burning converted merchantman which had performed exactly the same duty as a depot ship twenty-five years before, in the Great War. Painted an unlovely dirty grey, she was anchored out in the centre of the fiord. The *Emma* approached her rather like a toy boat, for the Base ship, although only single-funnelled like the trawler, was some thirty times her size.

After the *Emma* had tied up alongside they discovered that the inside of the Base ship was far more welcoming than her dismal outward appearance. There were hot showers, a ship's

81

barber constantly on duty, and a big canteen with a counter at which ratings queued to buy their ration of cigarettes, tobacco, sweets – and oranges, a surprise treat long since reserved at home for mothers-to-be and babies.

'Oranges! If only I could post some back to my missus.'

'What – is she expecting *again*?'

'Some hopes, with her there and me out here!'

It was James who soon found that there was an evening film show in the torpedo flat.

'James Cagney,' he said delightedly. 'Bang-bang! Okay, Pricey?'

'Sorry, I've got to see the Buffer, and I'm down for Quartermaster.'

The glass had fallen steeply. The duty seamen had been warned to watch the weather as it might blow up, but, seeing that they were tucked away in a sheltered fiord, they did not think the weather would worry them overmuch. However, by the time Price went on watch at midnight it was blowing hard and increasing. Sub-Lieutenant Grant, the duty officer, decided that he and Price had better put out some more wires and ropes to the Base ship, but in the wind they had difficulty in getting anyone on board the big vessel to hear their shouts. At last they did manage to make themselves heard and extra ropes were secured, but ten minutes later there was more trouble. Two more trawlers had tied up to the Base ship outboard of the *Lady Emma* and the stern wire of the one nearest to her parted. While Grant and Price, helped by the vessel's Quartermaster, were fixing another wire, the trawler's wire on the *Emma*'s bow also parted. Grant and Price rushed for'ard to the foc'sle, where the wind, now risen to gale force, buffeted them almost off their feet. They flung heaving lines across, but the wind carried them away. The other Quartermaster seemed unable to rouse either crew or an officer, and in answer to Grant's urgent shouts could only shrug his shoulders helplessly.

Grant swore. Suddenly the breast-ropes gave way and both the other trawlers were in danger of being swept away.

'Price – go below and rouse the duty watch!' Grant shouted.

He raced down and shook the others out of their warm bunks, which they left reluctantly and with loud protests. Then they were all at it, throwing heaving lines, passing ropes and wires and heaving on winches to bring the ships together again. The next-door trawler's Quartermaster had at last succeeded in raising some of his hands and one very disgruntled officer to whom Grant, rising strongly to the occasion and heedless of the other's rank, delivered a censure in the most expressive Naval terms. Then, to cap it all, the outboard trawler started parting her wires and ropes.

'Shit!'

The gale was screaming down the fiord and they could hardly stand or make their voices heard across the ships as they worked, cutting their numbed hands on wires and stumbling blindly over obstructions on deck. They hoped the duty watch on the Base ship would be roused to come up and lend a hand, but that vessel remained as silent as the dead. They battled on.

When Price turned in he looked at his watch. It was 5.30 a.m. He and Grant had had five and a half hours of it.

It seemed he had hardly closed his eyes before the day Quartermaster's voice bellowed down the messdeck hatch, 'Price! Report to Lieutenant Hadley in the Wardroom!'

Bleary with unfinished sleep he stumbled his way to the holy-of-holies, took off his cap, knocked and entered.

'Ordinary-Seaman Price reporting, sir.'

'Price, I take it you would prefer to be "Seaman Price"?'

'Yes, sir.'

'Then take this paper. There are six questions on it. Write down the answers and report to me on the foc'sle in twenty minutes sharp.'

'Yes, sir.'

'The correct response to an *order*, Price, is "Aye, aye, sir".'

'Yes, sir. I mean, aye, aye, sir!'

His head clearing, he raced away and studied the paper. They were simple questions from the Seamanship Manual, which he easily answered, and he timed himself to appear on the foc'sle to the second. The wind had dropped, but it was raw cold. Hadley, on being handed the completed paper, gave it a cursory glance and beckoned him along the deck, giving him verbal instructions. While the No. 1 stomped around with an air of utter boredom Price, as ordered, tied some sailor's knots, threw heaving lines and secured rope around bollards with hands cut and chafed from his work the night before.

'Mr Grant tells me that you know your Manual?'

'Yes, sir. That is, I've studied it.'

Hadley stomped some more against the cold and rapped out a few questions on sound and light signals by vessels, and the differences in hemp, sisal and coir rope and when to use each.

He hardly seemed to take notice of the answers, but Price knew that he did in fact register every word.

'Very well. I shall now enter you for Seaman.'

'Thank you, sir.'

Hadley nodded airily, as if the whole chilly business had been an unwarranted intrusion upon his precious time. Then his grey eyes suddenly met those of Price challengingly.

'What would you do if I fell overboard?'

'Shout "Man overboard!", throw a line and dive in after you, sir.'

'You would? That's an unusual lower-deck reaction, isn't it?' he said sarcastically.

'I don't know, sir.'

Hadley allowed the glimmer of a smile to light up his bored, handsome face.

'Price, you will be shot at until you reach King Alfred, and when you get there you might wish you had not. The path of a C.W. candidate can be a very thorny one.'

'I understand that, sir.'

'Do you? Which bank did you work for?'

Price told him.

'Hmm. Not mine,' said Hadley, thinking ruefully of his overdraft. 'My recommendation will go ashore to be ratified by the N.O.I.C. That is all.'

'Thank you, sir.'

As the No. 1 walked away James sauntered across the deck.

'Congratulations, Seaman Price.'

'Thank you, Seaman Crawford.'

'Just think, one day you might be knocking back the gin with our Mr Hadley.'

'I can't imagine it.'

'Maybe not,' said James, 'but he can. Don't underestimate him. He's no fool to have reached such a perfect understanding with a rough diamond like McBride. R.N.R. and R.N.V.R. – never the twain shall meet, they say. But those two, poles apart as they are, have come pretty close to it.'

'Is that the end of the lesson?'

'Yes. I've got an ucker board, dear boy. You know, halma – "uckers". Now we can play a real Naval game – almost makes us one of the Fleet.'

'Where did you get it?'

'From the padre.' James nodded towards the Base ship. 'He's got a huge store of comforts – up to his ears in indoor games.

Ginger and Eddie have come back loaded – cards, draughts, even a dart board. It's going to be a barrel of fun.'

'Any news of what's going to happen to us?'

'No. But the Old Man and Hadley are going ashore this afternoon.'

It was a day of comings and goings, and any doubts that still existed about their going on convoy were dispelled the next morning when the *Lady Emma* detached from the Base ship and moved over to a collier.

As they approached, big Ginger cupped his hands and shouted, 'Is there a bottom?'

'No, mate.'

The *Lady Emma*'s crew groaned. With no 'bottom' to the coal in the collier their work would be doubly hard. And so it proved. There was no friendly grab. They had to go down into the collier's hold, dig the coal out for themselves, shovel it into three-quarter ton buckets, winch the buckets across to the *Emma* and empty them on deck, then fill the trawler's bunkers. It was a tedious and back-breaking process with one party busy in the collier's hold, another working on the trawler's deck, and the stokers trimming it into the bunkers.

As the first of the great buckets swung over from the collier Ginger spat and fixed his eye on Price.

'Remember two things, lad. Never stand near a taut wire or under a swinging load. When a taut wire snaps it can cut a man in half – I've seen it happen. Same with a swinging load – if the wire breaks and you're under that bloody lot, you end up just a mangled pulp. So if you want to stay alive, mate – watch it!'

They worked all day, two hours on, two hours off, until they were as black as night. When the bunkers were full to over-flowing more coal was heaped for passage on the trawler's deck. Never had they taken so much coal on board; it was going to be a long, long journey. McBride was still ashore, but Lieutenant Hadley, who had returned to the ship, spent a considerable time wielding a shovel; they were coaling to a new purpose now. During the long operation a roar of mingled delight and derision went up from one side of the ship and was then quickly hushed as Hadley investigated. Sub-Lieutenant Sibley emerged on deck limping badly and, grim-faced, stumbled away to the Ward-room. He had stepped backwards into an open coal-hole, fallen down the bunkers and injured a leg.

'Silly bastard!' said Eddie Nash viciously. 'Goes around

spouting K.R. and A.I. and can't do a simple navvying job without making a bleedin' mess of it.'

Price could not help feeling sorry for the man. If anyone needed a friend it was Arthur Sibley. The final straw which had turned the crew's contempt for him into a common hatred had occurred shortly before Price joined the *Emma*. In every ship, one of the officers had the none too welcome task of censoring the crew's letters home; it was generally considered an embarrassing duty and for this reason it was not disclosed to the messdeck which officer actually did the censoring. Secrets like this, however, could not be kept for long on board a small ship like the *Lady Emma* with such a wide-awake Wardroom steward as Jerry Baxter. The news that Sibley was the censor had been received with a wave of disgust. The thought that this detestable man could, and did, read their most tender intimacies on paper, to wives, fiancées or girl friends had filled the crew with impotent rage. Wherever possible they tried to post their letters ashore.

After the coaling, which was not finished until the following day, lighters began to arrive with stores and ammunition. Grant put Price in charge of an unloading party which included Ginger Meeson, and the big man, as he handled sacks and boxes effortlessly, looked at Price giving directions with eyes alive with amusement.

Willie the Buffer brought news from the Coxswain. 'Any mon with an old or damaged watchcoat can exchange it for a new duffle coat from the Base ship stores. Report to the Cox'n within the next hour.'

Men fell to and examined their leather coats.

'No good,' said Ted Beckles. 'Cox'n'll say mine's got another two years' life in it yet.'

'Chuck it over to me a minute,' said Ginger. He opened the coat out on his bunk and examined it carefully.

'I'd say this coat was well and truly buggered,' he pronounced gravely. Whipping out his seaman's knife he slashed the coat with a few deft strokes, threw it over to Beckles and rolled back on his bunk shrieking with laughter.

In a matter of seconds knives were produced all over the messdeck and there was a sound of rending and tearing as all the better looking coats received well delivered gashes up and down their lengths.

When they reported to Coxswain Reid he dourly took each man's coat and tossed it into a growing heap of discarded garments, stopping every now and then to inspect the more obvious knife-marks but making no comment and, without a flicker of an eyelid, checking each name off a list.

'Price, Brewster, your coats.'

They handed them to him, embarrassed in front of the others that they had demurred against using their knives to further spoil the coats, which were second-hand when they had received them. But the Coxswain simply threw them on to the pile with the others.

'Right, a duffle coat for every man. Also fleece-lined oilskins, seaboots – take the rest of your old gear to the Base ship's stores to hand over in exchange.'

Later they trooped back to the *Emma* laden with new gear and walked about getting the feel of their khaki-coloured duffle coats, or 'duffield' coats as the scrawny McDougal called them. He had never looked so alarmingly smart. And big Ginger, in his duffle, looked twice as enormous.

'Now we're all officers,' said Beckles.

'All we need is our half boots,' agreed Sam the fisherman.

'What we *really* need,' said Jack Barrow, 'is some more warm gear for *up there*.' He flung out an arm dramatically in the direction of unknown northern seas.

'What about those kapok zip-up suits the destroyer lads wear?' Beckles suggested.

'If you want those,' said Eddie Nash, 'you'll have to join the bleedin' Navy – not this Harry Tate's outfit.'

The Quartermaster's face appeared at the messdeck hatch. 'Working party!'

They tumbled on deck to find a lighter arrived and its crew in the process of swinging on board six hefty crates, which were to be stacked on the trawler's deck.

'Comforts for the bloody Russians,' said Tilson.

They secured the crates, on each of which was stencilled, in big black letters, 'MURMANSK'. With a jolt they realised the nature of their imminent voyage, its drama heightened by the fact that none of them knew the whereabouts of the name emblazoned starkly on the crates.

'Where is Murmansk?' asked Brewster when he returned to the messdeck with Price and James.

'I expect they're puzzling that one out in the Wardroom,' James replied. 'But we can solve it just as well. Hold on.'

He dived across to his bunk and returned with a tattered six-penny school atlas.

'Now let's see . . . there she blows. Murmansk – up round Norway and first turning on the right past Finland.'

'It doesn't look all that far away,' said Brewster, relieved.

'That's right,' said James. 'Only about two thousand miles from Iceland. A piece of cake.'

'I wonder how we'll get there?'

'I'm guessing,' said James, 'but there seems to be only one way for us. Look, we're down here in south-west Iceland. I reckon we'll go up the west coast of Iceland, turn round at the top and go north-eastwards past Jan Mayen Island and on past Bear Island into the Barents Sea. After that, Bob's your uncle and down to Murmansk. That is, if there's no one there to try to stop us.'

'What do you mean?'

'Jerry planes, my son. They fly out from Norway. Torpedo-carrying planes, our Base ship brothers say. And U-boats.'

'What – in those icy waters?'

'Yes. They have specially frozen German crews.'

'From what I've heard,' said Price, 'the crews are pretty lively.'

'Some say the U-boats hide under the edge of the polar ice barrier waiting for convoys,' said Ted Beckles.

'Rubbish,' said James. 'Jules Verne stuff. They'll have them crawling about the ice on legs next – like giant crabs.'

'They also say there's a lot of German spies in Iceland who give Berlin the tip-off about our convoys.'

'That's possible.'

'What about the Jerry battleship – the *Tirpitz*? She's hiding up in Norway somewhere.'

'And don't forget the mermaids armed with machine-guns,' said James.

'Get stuffed!'

James scooped up his atlas. 'Well, chaps, we've always got the old spud-thrower. That puts us one up for a start.'

Price went up on deck. It was growing still colder and even the seawater began to freeze on deck where it landed. From his vantage point at the rail he saw some Icelandic fishing boats come in, looking like the frosted decorations seen on top of a wedding cake.

A drifter arrived alongside and delivered two men who came on board with their kit and were taken down to the messdeck by Nash, the Quartermaster. When Price went below he found that the identities of the newcomers had been speedily estab-

88

lished. They were extra crewmen for the Arctic voyage, a signalman and a telegraphist. Up till now on Northern Patrol the *Emma* had only ever carried one signalman, Bob Garrett, and one telegraphist, Tom Knox, each having a special independence in their roles. They kept watches at specified times, with intervals for rest, and maintained all their own gear; Knox, at the wireless, had to do all his own coding and de-coding of messages. But now, on convoy, they would each need a deputy so that continuous watches could be kept.

The new men were both aged around twenty. The signalman's name was Boone. He was sharp-faced with slicked-back hair, his skin waxen and eyes very bright. He had come from a pleasure paddle-steamer, the *Western Belle*, now converted to an anti-aircraft ship.

'We might be paddling this lousy old tub before we're through,' said Tilson gloomily.

The telegraphist, named Shelley, had come from a mine-sweeping trawler. He was fair-haired and good-looking, and seemed easy natured and to 'know the ropes'. But one item of his kit drew caustic comment.

'Are we taking on bloody musicians now?' asked Ginger.

Shelley laughed and took his ukulele out of its case.

'I'll bet you're a real George Formby,' grunted Barrow.

'Well,' said Shelley, 'I try.'

That night he entertained them with some Formby songs, pulling his rubbery face into a remarkable likeness of the toothy comedian.

Big Ginger was foremost among those joining in the chorus of 'When I'm Cleaning Windows' when Jerry Baxter came in, having finished his duties in the Wardroom. The steward sat down and waited till the song had ended. Then –

'It's tomorrow, lads,' he said. 'We sail tomorrow.'

And nobody yet had told them where.

9

There was an air of bustle and activity in the fiord. Merchant ships were heaving up their anchors and a handful of Naval escorts were fussing around. Finally, led by a smart escort sloop, the merchantmen lumbered towards the boom and passed through it in slow procession. Two minesweeper escorts moved off and the *Lady Emma* and another trawler, the *Melrose*, brought up the rear. It all took a long, wearisome time.

At last all the ships of the convoy were out in the open sea, wallowing in a heavy swell under a leaden, overcast sky. It was cold and dismal and cheerless. Signal lamps flashed and flag hoists went up as gradually the disposition of the convoy took shape. The fast sloop, which had herded the merchantmen into their respective stations like a busy sheepdog, flashed 'Good luck' to the *Lady Emma* and with a thresh of her tail departed for the head of the convoy. Eventually the columns of vessels moved off and began to settle down to a steady six knots, with some ships still ponderously weaving and skewing to achieve their proper stations.

From now on wireless silence had to be strictly observed and the *Emma*'s 'Sparkers', in common with the wireless operators on other ships of the convoy, would keep only a listening watch.

The jagged Icelandic coast was greyly discernible as the *Lady Emma* steamed at the starboard rear flank of the convoy, with the *Melrose* over on the port flank, but the weather was already deteriorating fast with a nagging, bitter wind gathering force, so no one stayed on deck who could avoid it.

James clattered down the messdeck ladder and struck a dramatic pose. 'A message from your captain,' he announced.

90

'Well, chaps, we're bound for Russia. It's going to be a hard, dangerous and uncomfortable voyage – and I want you all to do your damndest and pull together. Remember, we're a *team*. So chins up – and let's show 'em what the old *Emma* can do!'

He skilfully dodged a seaboot which was hurled at him and threw up a scornful hand against the heated flow of curses that followed in its wake. 'Rhubarb, rhubarb, rhubarb.' He strolled over and sat down beside Price. 'As our esteemed officers have seen fit to tell us precisely damn all,' he said, 'I thought one of us ought to do it for them.'

Price was silent. The absence of any word from the Wardroom was disappointing and, to him, quite wrong. There seemed no need for further secrecy now they were at sea, and a brief word from the C.O. would have helped uplift their low morale. But then this was the Patrol Service – 'Harry Tate's lot' – the rough and ready navy within the Navy which worked in makeshift ways peculiar to itself, much to the disdain and frequent disgust of the 'pusser' R.N.

'When you're dashing about in your destroyer,' said James, who seemed to guess what Price was thinking, 'I hope you'll make a point of keeping your men informed. They do, you know, in the real Navy. In the big ships they even have a Schoolmaster to explain to them what's going on. Now that's an officer rank that intrigues me. "Schoolmaster". I wonder if they give you a few sums to go along with every lesson – and perhaps a bit of homework besides?'

'That'll be the day when they tell *us* what's going on,' said Ted Beckles acidly.

'I can tell you what's going on,' said Jack Barrow. 'Cross-Buckets is throwing up his bloody guts again.'

'I hope he bleedin' chokes,' said Eddie Nash, still with a noxious smell in his nostrils after doing duty as a 'Chain-Locker Charlie'.

The melancholy Sibley was on the bridge when Price went on watch in the early hours of the night. A gale was now blowing, bringing heavy snow which quickly froze as it collected on the side of the ship. Because of a rearranged watch Price had to serve two hours' continuous for'ard lookout duty on the bridge wing. This was little more than a wooden box in which he could move only one pace, unlike on patrol, when a lookout could stamp around the bridge verandah to keep warm. The snow freezing fast to the *Emma*'s side also froze on his balaclava and duffle coat; he could even feel it freezing on his eyelashes. He kept shaking off the snow and stamping his feet in an effort to keep warm, but as time went by he gave this up and sank into a frozen numbness while the whole of his right side became whiter and whiter ...

All seemed quiet in the convoy, with the looming shapes ahead in the darkness steaming in fairly orderly fashion and the small, dim blue stern lights of the nearest vessels keeping an even distance from the trawler. Price nursed the hope that Sibley would invite him into the glass-protected comfort of the bridge-house for a brief spell, as was done on patrol in very severe weather. He brightened as eventually Sibley, still limping from his coaling accident and his face a peculiar pallor from constant visits to the sick-bucket, came out and peered over the side.

'My God, Price, have you seen this?'

'Yes, sir, I've seen it,' he replied without enthusiasm.

'It certainly is bad tonight. We have never been like this before.'

'No, sir?'

'No, Price. *Never*.'

Sibley winced as his troubled stomach rumbled and he walked quickly back into the comfort of the bridge, rubbing his hands against the cold. A few moments later he tapped on the glass and beckoned Price inside. Ah, thought the frozen lookout, he's taken pity on me at last. He went thankfully to the door and entered.

'Price,' Sibley snapped, 'the spray is going down the Ward-room ventilator – go down and turn it round the other way.'

Dispiritedly he trudged down and struggled with the rusted-in ventilator, getting soaked through by showers of spray before returning to his icy post, and when Sibley later sent him down to make kye he brought it up lukewarm, remaining stolidly un-moved by the No. 2's protests.

Next day the convoy pushed steadily on around the snow-bound Icelandic coast, battling through frequent snowstorms. Fog and icy winds tearing into their faces made it difficult for the *Lady Emma*'s muffled lookouts to keep their eyes open, while frozen snow had to be scraped regularly from the bridge windows. As the snowstorms continued banks of fog hung over the convoy, forcing all ships to stream fog-buoys. Station-keeping became increasingly more difficult and when night fell the hazards stepped up ten-fold. Anxious eyes strained to keep sight of the blue stern lights of vessels closest to them. Twice a wayward merchantman on the port bow came dangerously close to the *Emma*, the situation being saved each time by McBride's quick and sure commands. He stayed grimly on the bridge throughout the night, his presence keeping the watch on their mettle and a firm step away from panic. Wally Winters, on the wheel during the danger moments, was calmness itself. Then again the erratic merchantman bucked crazily across almost in front of the trawler.

'Ship coming close on port side!'

'Hard-a-starboard!'

This time they avoided the dark shape by a matter of yards.

'Who the hell is she?' asked Ted Beckles angrily.

'The *Wesleydale*, out of Liverpool.' Eddie Nash had just returned after gleaning the information from the signalman.

'A bloody Scouse,' said Jack Barrow the Liverpudlian disgustedly, without batting an eyelid. 'That captain shouldn't be allowed on the Mersey.'

Wally Winters shook his head in some sympathy with the vessel they had narrowly avoided. 'Not one of these ships has ever sailed in these waters before.'

'And a right scruffy lot of tramps some of them are,' said Eddie Nash. 'Have you seen that dirty old wreck on the seaward flank? I wouldn't use her to boil water in.'

'There's nothing wrong with the Merchant Navy lads themselves,' said Winters quietly. 'Isn't that so, Jack?'

Barrow, the long-serving peacetime seaman scowled. 'Maybe. But you don't get to choose your skippers, and I've sailed with some bloody fools in my time. Master mariners? I wouldn't give 'em command of the New Brighton ferry.'

Price and Brewster, off-watch together, sat at the roaring messdeck fire. Brewster was striving to put in order what Price had just told him.

'So, the Commodore of the convoy, in one of the merchantmen, gives orders by signal hoist to all the other ships?'

'Yes. And at night by signal lights – relayed down the columns of ships.'

'And the Commodore isn't Navy?'

'Well, he could be – perhaps a retired Admiral brought back into service. But he's more likely to be a senior merchant officer of the Royal Naval Reserve.'

'And one of the skippers of the other merchant ships is Vice-Commodore?'

'Yes. Just in case.'

'And the senior Naval escort agrees orders with the Commodore?'

'Yes, that's as far as I know. You've got it.'

'Seems simple enough.'

'It would be, if the weather didn't get in the way.'

'How many merchant ships did Bunts say there were?'

'About twenty-seven.'

Brewster looked deep into the dancing flames, and they were both conscious for a moment of the persistent whining noise from the small Asdic cabin on the messdeck which housed the alternator. 'You know, Peter,' he said, 'I'm glad we've got McBride.'

'So am I.'

The convoy rounded the North Cape of Iceland and steamed due north-east. The weather grew even worse, and a day of murk and sleet showers was followed by a night of vile visibility with McBride remaining tired-eyed on the bridge. The *Emma* was involved in another near-collision, this time with an unidentified ship that weaved dangerously across her path without warning. The trawler sounded her steam whistle in short, urgent blasts and McBride gave swift orders. They escaped hitting the other vessel by only a few feet – a nightmarish incident which had the duty watch oozing the sweat of fear beneath their duffle coats.

It was a long, long night. When daylight broke and the murk lifted it was to reveal the surprising sight of the *Emma* and six merchantmen steaming alone in a waste of grey sea. The rest of the convoy had vanished.

McBride and Hadley searched the surface of the ocean with their binoculars and went into consultation over the chart table. Then the larger of the merchant ships began signalling.

'I – am – ordering – all – ships – to – return – to – Iceland.'

McBride coughed and spluttered in his anger. 'Send the Vice-Commodore, "Our duty is to keep on course," ' he commanded.

Garrett despatched the message. After a short interval the Vice-Commodore replied. 'We – have – lost – the – convoy – my – duty – is – to – return – and – re-form.'

McBride banged his fist down hard on the chart table. 'Bunts! Tell him, "We can follow convoy at seven knots plus and rendezvous – see Convoy Orders paragraph seven." '

On receipt of this message there was a longer pause from the merchantman. Then her lamp blinked out again. 'I – am – ordering – all – ships – to – return – I – expect – you – to – escort – me.'

McBride angrily paced the bridge, muttering under his breath.

'He has the authority, sir – unfortunately,' Hadley quietly reminded him.

McBride stood with his hands clasped behind his back, glowering from the bridge window at the Vice-Commodore's ship sailing at the head of the depleted flock.

'Signalman, send "I comply".'

Immediately afterwards the flag hoists went up on the Vice-Commodore's ship and all vessels began to turn about.

On board the *Lady Emma* they spent the freezing morning chipping ice. The gun-crew had to chip it off the barrel, the breech block, the loading and firing mechanism; everywhere. Everything that did not move had rapidly iced up.

'Well, lads, that's the end of our convoy to Russia!'

'*Now* we'll get some bloody shore leave.'

'We might go for a refit. They'll have all the escorts they want lined up for the next convoy. They won't want us.'

'Some hopes. I wouldn't pack your suitcase.'

'Just let me get ashore at Iceland for a look at those gorgeous blondes.'

'That's all you're likely to get, mate – a look.'

In the afternoon the alarm-bells clanged twice, the alert for an unidentified aircraft. The plane was soon established to be British, a Hudson of Coastal Command. It flew over the small convoy signalling furiously.

'It's wondering what the bleedin' 'ell we're doing,' said Eddie Nash, 'seeing as Russia's the other way.'

Eventually the plane was satisfied and circled round and flew off.

'We're making for Akureyri,' Bob Garrett told them. 'A Naval base in the north of Iceland.'

By evening they were steaming up a placid fiord. The weather had made one of its lightning changes and the sun was shining, the air still and the atmosphere crystal clear. It was nearly 8 p.m. when they approached a small island on which there appeared to be a collection of military huts; but as the *Lady Emma* closed in they discovered that the 'huts' were the houses of the most picturesque village anyone had ever seen. Nestling beneath a background of towering, white-clad hills, the houses were painted all the colours of the rainbow. In the centre, standing alone in its quaint beauty, was a miniature church, looking straight out of Grimm's fairy tales, its dazzling whiteness topped by a spire of vivid scarlet. The crew stood at the ship's rail and gazed spellbound on the loveliness of this unexpected jewel shining among the rugged desolation. People could be seen walking about the village and such was the clarity of the air that although they were more than half a mile away they could catch the sound of the villagers' voices.

'It's a dream – pinch me,' said James.

When all the ships of the remnant convoy had let go their anchors, out came the fishing lines. Over the side from the *Lady Emma*'s rail they went, hand-made lines of twine and wire, their hooks baited with bits of meat and bread or some other tried and tested speciality of their owners. In the clear water the fish could be seen swimming around and the *Emma*'s crew hung over the rail willing them to bite, which they did almost immediately, the lines coming up with amazing rapidity. There were fine catches of mackerel, herring and whiting, but also of dogfish or 'bigheads', which were disgustedly unhooked and thrown back. The mournful McDougal caught all 'bigheads', much to Ginger's noisy amusement, but Wally Winters quietly saw to it that McDougal got his share of the eatable kind of fish. The cook would soon be busy serving up a welcome change of diet.

In the general activity little notice was taken of a boat which was being rowed across from the port's examination vessel in the flat calm. It contained the rower and a young sub-lieutenant who clambered on board the *Lady Emma*, climbed to the bridge and importantly approached McBride. Producing an official clip-board he attempted to ask the routine questions, 'How long are you staying? Are you sending anybody ashore?' but got short shrift as the irate Skipper proceeded to wither his tender ears with vitriolic comments on the dangerous recalcitrance and truculence of certain senior officers in merchant convoy and their doubtful parentage.

An exchange of lamp signals had begun between the Vice-Commodore's ship and the shore station. Garrett read the messages, which he pencilled down and handed to McBride. The first of them began bluntly, 'Why have you become detached?' The mischievous glint returned to McBride's eyes as he read on, and in better humour he stepped out on to the bridge verandah with Garrett and waited as the signalman read the latest signal to the Vice-Commodore's ship as it was flashed angrily from the shore.

'You – are – instructed – to – sail – forthwith – and – rendez-vous – convoy – at – Position X.'

McBride chuckled and Hadley nodded knowingly. They waited for the deflated Vice-Commodore to swallow his pride and relay the shore message to them in his own words. When it was received, McBride said, 'Send "I acknowledge that we are *now* to rejoin the convoy – your escort is ready".'

It was 10pm when the sailing orders were flashed, just two hours after their arrival. Anchors were weighed and they were off once more, except for two of the merchantmen who had, strangely, developed 'engine trouble' and resisted all attempts to get them moving.

'Crafty bastards!' said Jack Barrow suspiciously.

Disappointment was keen on board the *Lady Emma*, with all hopes of shore leave now sadly abandoned as the trawler and her flock of four remaining merchant ships steamed away into the darkening Arctic night.

The weather held fine throughout the night and was followed by an equally mellow dawn streaked with vivid colour, the sea remaining graciously calm. As they pushed on northwards they began to pass drifting pieces of scattered ice which grew more numerous as the day wore on. The erratic weather broke suddenly; a keen wind began searching and clawing at the decks and the idle sea became lively enough to send Sub-Lieutenant Sibley hastening to his bucket. In no time at all grey masses of snowstorms bore down on them across the water, blanketing the five vessels in a swirling whiteness.

'Merry Christmas,' said James cheerfully as he came to relieve Price on for'ard lookout.

'Wait,' said Price, peering intently through the snow shower. Then, 'Ship approaching on starboard bow! No – two ships!'

The alarm-bells clanged, but the vessels were soon identified. They were merchantmen which had turned back from the convoy. Only as the two drew closer did they see that one of them had a gaping black hole in her bows, a sombre sight.

The undamaged ship blinked a warning to the trawler. 'Bad – ice – ahead.' Then she very quickly added, 'Lost – convoy – can – I – join – you?'

McBride nodded and Hadley dictated a signal in reply, 'Glad to have you join the dance.'

The merchantman turned and took up station, leaving her damaged companion to continue a slow passage back to Iceland, the captain having indicated that he was in no immediate need of assistance.

Six ships now, they pressed on. James's breezy voice sang out on lookout and again the bells clanged, but it was yet another straggler from the convoy homeward bound, presumably having also retreated from the menacing ice. Despite repeated flashing from Bob Garrett her captain seemed too disgruntled even to answer the *Lady Emma*'s signals and the ship receded into the distance followed by some acrimonious remarks from McBride.

They were now dodging small patches of pack ice, and when darkness came it brought more squally snow showers together with all the accumulated muck of the heavens, reducing visibility to less than two hundred yards. Once again the lookouts' eyes ached in their search to pin-point elusive blue stern lights. Ice bumped and thumped its way alarmingly along the trawler's side, making sleep impossible.

'Here, Pricey, have a read,' said James encouragingly, tossing him a book. 'Chekhov. Anton Pavlovich to you, that well known Russian. T'will tickle your think-box and make a change from your Manual.'

But Price could not read. He was due on watch at 4 a.m., but with less than an hour to go the alarm-bells clanged a series of three – submarine alert. He hurled himself up on deck with the others, hardly anyone pausing to grab a coat. Going from the warmth of the messdeck into the Arctic night, the cold struck them like a blow. The four-inch men climbed the ladder up to the whaleback and huddled round the gun, knees knocking, teeth chattering. They were given a bearing, swung the gun round on it and placed ammunition on the tray.

Lieutenant Hadley, well muffled up against the weather, looked them over pityingly and spoke briskly to 'Guns', who then instructed them to dash smartly down, one at a time, and put on woollens and duffle coats; they could not have withstood the intense cold for long without proper protection.

For half an hour men remained at their posts, then action-stations were secured. The for'ard lookout had reported a submarine shape in the misty dark, but it was probably no more than a large piece of ice; the night was full of such ghostly shapes. As it was now practically time for his watch Price went up to the bridge wing and took over from Jack Barrow.

'That bastard Sibley told me to get shaved,' said Barrow,

rubbing a bristly chin. 'I hope he drowns in his bucket. If I had a hold of his head I'd see to it he did.'

The mist had now turned to thick fog. Normally, in such conditions, the *Lady Emma*'s speed would have been reduced to dead-slow, but such was the need for haste to catch the convoy that her engines were kept thumping away at full speed. There was still plenty of ice about and the trawler edged her way through it at seemingly breakneck speed. All that could be seen of the merchant ships was the looming hull of the vessel on the port beam when she closed in on them, so close that twice the *Emma* had to go hard-a-starboard to avoid collision.

Straining the eyes to peer into bad fog at night could cause a lookout after a time to conjure up shapes of things that were not really there, as had happened over the 'submarine'. After being on lookout for nearly an hour Price saw to his astonishment what appeared to be the end of the sea a hundred yards ahead. The sea just seemed to finish there, beyond was nothingness – it was as though the horizon had been telescoped right up close to the ship. For a mad couple of seconds he had the nightmarish fancy that they were running off the edge of the world and would topple down into yawning space. Then he saw the nothingness was really something and another horrible thought struck him, causing him to yell out with the full force of his lungs: 'Land ahead!'

But it was too late to take the way off the ship and she hit with a rending crash that jarred her from stem to stern. It was not land, thank God, it was a big ice floe – part of a huge field of ice shrouded in the ghostly fog. He felt sure that the *Emma* must have had every rivet torn out of her and he could imagine those below leaping wildly from their bunks. But the trawler survived the mighty crash and she was not holed.

'Stop engines!'

The silent *Emma* wallowed blindly in the dark, frozen field, an experience even more unnerving than her collision with the giant floe. When the fog shifted slightly they could just glimpse through the vaporous banks the merchantmen pushing on through the ice; being more strongly built they kept their engines turning and were soon swallowed up in the darkness. The *Emma* drifted on through the floes, started up her engines again, but then ran into more dark floes and stopped again; McBride was taking few chances.

In this fashion the trawler made slow progress through the night, with the constant sound of loose ice banging against her sides, disturbing the sleepers on the messdeck, who dozed uneasily with heads lolling foolishly and mouths open.

When daylight came it revealed the *Lady Emma* steaming alone in a sea of ice stretching as far as the eye could see.

10

'What I'd like to know,' said Ted Beckles, 'is what we're doing steaming so far north. Why we're going up against all this ice.'

'Don't you know?' said Eddie Nash. 'The Old Man's looking for the North Pole.'

'If we keep on like this,' said Tommy Tilson, 'we're bloody well going to find it. What do you say, Wally?'

Winters blew into his frozen hands and pulled on his working gloves.

'Mac knows his business,' he said. 'Seems to me the convoy is travelling high to the north so as to keep a good distance between us and Norway – and the Jerry planes.'

'It would make more sense to me,' said Jack Barrow, 'if we went south out of this lousy ice and clapped on a few knots. We can't keep up with those merchant buggers in this lot.'

'Even when we find them again,' agreed Beckles.

Price found James leaning over the port rail with a Woodbine dangling from his lips.

'Just think, Pricey, there's enough ice out there to fill a million fish shops – and plenty more to spare.'

'The fog's coming in again.'

'That's all we need,' sighed James, and intoned in a sepulchral voice, ' "Fair is foul, and foul is fair, hover through the fog and filthy air . . . " ' With leering face he stirred an invisible cauldron.

As the weather closed in, the *Lady Emma* began again the tedious routine of hopping, as it were, from floe to floe, McBride being acutely mindful of Chief Hook's snarled warning that this was the only way to proceed through the ice 'unless you want to lose your bloody prop.' As soon as the trawler was clear of one ice floe she steamed at full speed to the next, then stopped engines and drifted through.

When the fog lifted again it was possible to take a good look at the floes. They were in the form of an immense triangle, with the base to the north and thinning as they streamed away southwards; masses of closely-packed lumps of ice, each of which must have weighed many tons. The slight swell brought the nearest floes almost on to the *Emma*'s decks. If the sea had been at all rough they would have crushed the ship like matchwood, but there was now only the slightest of breezes. Seen at such close quarters the floes were more blue than white, fantastically shaped, often into the likeness of animals, and were carved by the sea into blue grottoes and caves.

It was a weird and desolate sight. Like the Ancient Mariner, they felt that they must be 'the first that ever burst into that silent sea'.

But there was some life out there. Occasionally they saw seals climbing on to the floes to ride along with them.

'Look,' said James, pointing to a large block of ice on which was rolling a pure white young seal, like a kitten at play.

'That's nothing,' said Nash. 'Geordie saw a walrus surface ahead.'

'What did it do?' asked Price.

'Gave a loud belch and submerged again. Probably got a good look at Geordie and had a hell of a fright.' Nash looked out at the playful young seal with a touch of despair. 'Next, it'll be rollicking big polar bears doing the bleedin' hokey-cokey on the big chunks.'

By the afternoon things had improved. The floes were more widely spaced and the lumps smaller. The *Lady Emma* maintained a steady passage and there was a sudden air of activity on the bridge, with McBride glued to his binoculars. Eddie Nash spread the news.

'Bunts says we're near the spot where we ought to meet the convoy.'

Off-duty men came up from the messdeck to join those working and watching. There was an air of curious expectancy about what they might see. A smudge of smoke, the shape of a ship, and then, perhaps, like a living scene with the enshrouding curtains of nature suddenly lifted aside, a familiar, friendly, orderly procession of ships.

'All right, lads,' announced Willie the Buffer, 'there's a tin of ticklers from Mr Hadley for the first man to spot the convoy.'

But it was not this promised prize of Navy tobacco that kept them searching the icy sea, it was the warming prospect of finding fellow souls in the vast emptiness.

Alastair the Stornowegian scanned the sea with his far-seeing blue eyes as keenly as a cut-throat razor whisking close to the skin. He spat every few minutes, for his stomach was giving trouble. Always quiet, Alastair had now become almost completely silent, as if strangely affected by the icefield. He would come down to the mess, eat his meal in silence and leave again without a word to anyone. All attempts to draw him out were unsuccessful and the only time his lips were seen to move was when he silently pored over his Bible in his bunk, laboriously mouthing every word. On duty he would just stare at everyone and everything as if constantly bemused. Nash would nudge Price at the mess table and say, 'Look at old Alastair, the happy old bleeder!' But the Stornowegian was anything but happy as he searched the Arctic wastes, for he alone of all the men on board had lived his life close to the hard northern seas, knew their frenetic and terrible moods, and remembered the tragic tales told among the fisher folk.

As time went by still without a sign of ship or smoke, Lieutenant Hadley came down from the bridge and joined Sibley for'ard on the well-deck, where the No. 2 was directing a working party of ice chippers. The two officers paced the deck together and sharp ears overheard snatches of their conversation. They were discussing the difficulties of navigation with no sun or stars from which to take sights, and the added complication of allowing for deviation of the magnetic compass, which was subject to irregularities in these high latitudes and was not helped by a possible change in the ship's magnetism due to the continued hammering of ice against her hull. However, they seemed agreed that, with everything considered, the ship must now be steaming in the area of Position X.

Their conversation ended, the two officers stood watching the working party, each full of their own thoughts. Suddenly Sibley looked up skywards, then turned to Hadley.

'We could get a better lookout from the crow's nest.'

The crew heard the suggestion with horror. They gazed up aghast at the crow's nest, which had up till now been looked on more in the light of an ornamental, rather than a practical, part of the *Emma*'s fittings. The 'ratlines' or tarred rope rungs by which one climbed up the mast stays to reach the lofty perch had not been renewed within memory and looked far too rotten to bear a man's weight. But clearly Sibley was full of the importance of his novel suggestion.

Hadley looked the No. 2 square in his pallid face. 'Yes,' he said slowly, 'it *is* a good idea.'

His eyes held Sibley's in a steady gaze, and the No. 2 was hotly conscious of their unmistakable message; indeed, their open challenge. An officer, said those cool grey eyes should give the lead to the crew, and that officer should be the one who had broached the idea.

Sibley sensed the alert, provocative air among the seamen who had stopped their ice chipping to see the next step in this unexpected little drama. He was aware of the quizzical look on the face of big Ginger Meeson, the slyly cocked head of the disreputable McDougal, the insolent stare of Jack Barrow. He would show them, once and for all. With set mouth and a determined hitch of his shoulders he walked purposefully across the deck, but before he could reach the ship's side Eddie Nash had rushed there before him.

'Aye, aye, sir!' shouted the Cockney as he jumped on to the rail and grabbed hold of the mast stay. Then he began to climb, testing each rope rung carefully before putting his weight on it, but making a quick and expert ascent as if he had done such a thing every day on the Thames barges. Watched breathlessly by all, he nimbly reached the top, clambered over the side of the barrel-shaped crow's nest and stood inside it, the side coming up to his chest. As everyone below gave an inward sigh of relief he looked cockily around the horizon with a hand shaded to his forehead like Robinson Crusoe on the hilltop of his island.

'Nothing, sir!' he yelled. 'There's nothing ahead but sea and ice!'

Big Ginger chuckled. Ted Beckles said, 'Well, there he is up in his nest. All it wants now is a bird to bring him a worm.'

'Talking of worms . . . ' added Jack Barrow. He jerked his head in the direction of Sub-Lieutenant Sibley, who throughout Nash's climb had remained grimly rooted to his spot on the deck. Now he turned abruptly and walked back to the bridge. The moment had been his, but he had lost. Nash's public revenge was complete.

Nash remained up aloft for half an hour before being called down by the Buffer. On reaching the deck he stamped and worked his frozen limbs, teeth chattering.

'That's the closest you'll get to heaven, Eddie boy,' said Beckles.

'It's too bleedin' cold for angels up there, mate,' replied Nash. He staggered as he was thumped in the back by smiling Paddy Kelly. 'That's me bhoy!' beamed the big stoker.

'Turn it up, you old peat-basher. Where's Cross-Buckets?'

'Sulking,' said Ginger. And his big frame began to shake and shake with gurgles of upsurging laughter.

By the afternoon the creeping fog had come again. It seemed to rise up in misty fingers from the sea as well as rolling in on all sides, until by early evening the *Lady Emma* was steaming slowly ahead completely blind.

'Listen!' Jack Barrow whipped off his gloves and cupped his hands to his ears. 'Do you hear it?'

Price strained his ears against the deadening fog but was conscious only of the trawler's own muffled noises.

'Quick, over to the starboard side,' said Barrow, and they ran to the rail and listened again. Then it came, weirdly and faintly out of the depths of the fog.

Wheeee-ew . . . wheeee-ew . . . It was the shrill whistle of a warship's siren. The bridge lookout had now heard it and there followed moments of tension while all speculated as to whether it was friend or foe. Then McBride, still weary-eyed at his post on the bridge, pulled the lanyard and the *Emma*'s steam whistle pumped out in morse her distinguishing call-sign.

After an anxious interval the other ship replied, still faint, giving her own call-sign.

'It's one of the minesweepers, boys!'

A cheer went up on deck but was quickly hushed as they strained their ears to hear more. The *Emma* blew her whistle again, and again the minesweeper replied. Then a third vessel joined in.

'The *Melrose*. We've found them!'

Again the *Emma* blew, and the other two ships replied. The exchanges continued for some time, but the whistles of the other vessels gradually became fainter and fainter, until at last they died away altogether and left the *Lady Emma* wrapped in fog and despairing silence. They had been friendly sounds, and now the trawlermen felt more alone than ever in the murky greyness.

On the bridge McBride and Hadley despondently consulted the charts and arrived at a mutual decision. Jerry the steward brought the tidings to the messdeck.

'We're going on. Mac's heading for the next point of rendezvous, Position Y.'

The ice thickened up and the *Emma* had to resort to her old tactics of floe-hopping. Price, on watch, felt a new extreme of deep, freezing cold creep through his clothing as it descended on the ship like an icy blanket; it deadened his very bones. His relief brought him the news that the stokers were complaining that the 'bloody engine room's all frozen up', a remarkable happening in that place of heat and steam. His watch over, Price thawed out his dulled and aching body beside the mess-deck fire and went groggily to his bunk. But sleep was impossible with the sound of ice bumping along the side of the ship.

He tried to remember the thickness of the steel which formed the hull of the *Lady Emma* – was it one-eighth or one-quarter of an inch? Whichever it was, it gave him a peculiar feeling to think that only this measurement separated him from the huge ice blocks that banged and bumped so close to him. Suppose that thin wall cracked from an extra big thump? He could picture the water pouring in and over them all. Better to keep the mind off such thoughts, so he picked up the Chekhov book which James had given him, 'The Cherry Orchard'.

He tried to read, then flipped the pages, sampling the play's dialogue with its unfamiliar appended stage instructions – '(Weeps.)' There seemed to be plenty of weeping going on. As he turned the pages a folded piece of paper fell out which he ignored at first, thinking it must have been used by James as a marker, but then he saw it was typewritten, and he opened and read it. It was headed 'Death is a Door, by Nancy Byrd Turner', and ran –

> 'Death is only an old door
>   Set in a garden wall.
> On gentle hinges it gives at dusk,
>   When the thrushes call.
> Along the lintel's green leaves
>   Beyond the light lies still.
> Very willing and weary feet
>   Go over that sill.
> There is nothing to trouble any heart,
>   Nothing to hurt at all.
> Death is only a quiet door
>   In an old wall.'

Looking across he saw James lying awake in his hammock, and took the paper to him.

'Oh, *that* – is that where it got to,' said James, clearly embarrassed. 'I pinched it out of some book.'

He stuffed the paper into a breast pocket and dismissed it.

'How are you getting on with Chekhov, chum?'

'There's an awful lot of weeping.'

'Yes. It's very Russian, you know.'

'Some day, James, I'll make you out.'

'That's the right officer-like mentality, Pricey,' James retorted delightedly. 'First get to know what makes your men tick!'

Price returned to his bunk and tried to doze, but all he could think of was a quiet door in an old wall, and a lot of weeping Russians. Absurdly it had not occurred to him before that stolid Russians might actually cry. Eventually, the constant banging of the ice receded from his ears as uneasy sleep took hold.

At midnight there was a great spine-jarring crash which seemed to stop the *Lady Emma* dead in her tracks. Everyone leapt from their bunks, fearing the worst. Hoarse shouts were heard from above and, led by Ernie Michael, a party of hands came clattering down the ladder and started to work feverishly over the well that housed the Asdic dome.

In answer to the many shouts of 'What's up?' the bearded H.S.D. turned and glared at them savagely.

'The bloody dome's gone – that's what!'

The Asdic dome, which protruded like a blister on the bottom of the hull, had been shorn off by the trawler's violent entry into an ice floe. Michael and his helpers worked fast to withdraw the internal mechanism and make sure that no leaks had been caused. The operation was speedily done without any assistance being needed from the men who were off-watch, and James was the first to climb back into bed, reading as he swung gently in his hammock. This was too much for a nervously excited stoker.

'Look at yon booger, reading a *book*, if you please, while the ship goes down!'

'My dear man,' replied James, 'if we are going down, which I very much doubt, I prefer to do it in comfort.'

A battery of protests fell about the bewildered stoker's head.

'Who's sinking?'

'Pessimistic bastard!'

'Call yourself a bleedin' sailor?'

'It's nobbut a bit of bloody ice, lad.'

107

But they were all well shaken and aware of the real situation arising from the accident. Without the dome the Asdic was useless; now they were 'blind' underwater as well as on the foggy surface.

The *Emma* restarted her engines, and as each man retreated silently into his own thoughts loose ice continued to bang its way along the ship's side and make settled sleep impossible. In his bunk above Price, Brewster was quietly re-reading one of Enid's letters. He had been very withdrawn during the work on the Asdic well and Price sensed his unspoken fears.

'Eric,' he said, 'promise me I won't have to make a speech.'

'What?'

'I don't like making speeches.'

Brewster's head peered down curiously. 'What are you talking about?'

'The wedding, you fool.'

'Oh.' Brewster came to life and smiled faintly. 'You're kidding me, Peter.'

'No speech, eh?'

'If there *is* a wedding.'

'Of course there's going to be a wedding. And I'll be keeping an eye on you with those Russian girls at Murmansk. No hanky panky, or else.'

'Do you really think we'll make it?'

'Make it? We must be nearly half-way there by now!'

Dawn brought a break in the fog, but no lessening of the general gloom that had descended on everyone following the crash in the night. There was none of the usual banter at breakfast, and Price was glad to finish his meal and be away. He went up to the wireless cabin to tell the two 'Sparkers' that their meal was waiting for them, but as soon as he opened the cabin door he realised that something was wrong, for instead of the usual hum and crackle all was utterly quiet. Tom Knox's balding head was bent intently over the transmitter, his brow creased with worry, while the new man, young Shelley, had in his hands what appeared to be a valve and some wiring. Both men, tired and strained, started up guiltily when he sang out, 'Breakfast!'

Knox nodded, and it was on the tip of Price's tongue to ask what the devil was the matter when Sub-Lieutenant Grant came up from behind and tapped him on the shoulder. When he turned, Grant beckoned him away from the cabin.

'Price, you have eyes, and I don't want this to get around the crew just yet. The wireless is temporarily out of order, but it's being repaired. Can you arrange, without fuss, for the telegraphists' meals to be brought up in the mess tins?'

'I'll do that, sir.'

'We must take care not to spread undue alarm.'

'I understand. Does this mean we can't receive any incoming signals?'

Grant weighed his answer carefully before replying, but having taken Price this far into his confidence he could not be evasive. 'That is the position – at the moment. I rely on you to keep this information strictly to yourself.'

'Yes, sir.'

He went down, swung a tale about tiredness and queasy stomachs and collected the telegraphists' meals from the mess-man, then handed them into the wireless cabin without comment, and afterwards returned to collect the plates and tins and take them to the mess.

'You're in the wrong job, Pricey – you'd make a fine steward,' said Beckles, having observed his busy errands.

'A better steward than he was a messman,' said big Ginger, chuckling. 'How about bringing me my breakfast in bed?'

'All right – if you leave me a good tip.'

Ginger shook with mirth. 'Oh, you're a right one, Pricey, you are.'

McBride remained chained to his post on the bridge. He had been provided with a chair and there he sat, haggard and heavy-eyed, nodding and dozing in spite of his best efforts to keep awake.

'I have ordered the watch, where possible, to describe the nature of the ice ahead, sir,' said Hadley. 'This will help us to avoid further trouble. I have spoken to Winters, who has some experience in these matters and will instruct the crew.'

'Good.' McBride roused himself to use his binoculars, and satisfied himself that the *Lady Emma* could take advantage of a temporary easing of the ice. 'Up ten turns.'

'Aye, aye, sir.'

Wally Winters took his job very seriously as he explained to groups of men the different kinds of ice. From his descriptions the mass of ice took on individual identities. They had never before realised that there were so many varieties of ice on the sea: the pack-ice of the floes, the large separated pieces which had to be dodged, the broken small-ice, pancake ice, mush ice, and poached egg ice, which looked for all the world like poached eggs perched on the top of the blocks. Then there were the occasional huge icebergs, solitary, majestic and towering, coloured in greens and blues, which had to be given a wide berth.

It was Barrow's voluntary turn up in the crow's nest, from where he bellowed down snatches of song and a running commentary.

'Oh, he flies through the air with the greatest of ease, that daring young man on the flying trapeze . . . Well, here we are, it's a lovely day everybody, I am speaking to you from the Royal box at Ascot and it's a grand sight . . .'

The return of the fog put a damper on things as the *Emma* was reduced to floe-hopping, stopping and starting her engines.

'The Chief says his boilers will burst if he gets much more of this,' said Eddie Nash.

'The Chief will say any bloody thing,' growled Tommy Tilson.

Beckles came clattering down the messdeck ladder. 'Bunts says we're getting close to Position Y.'

'We'll never find 'em in this pea-souper.'

'Balls! We found them once, we can do it again.'

'Aye, we only missed the boogers by inches.'

'If the fog lifts we'll do it.'

'I'm going up to have a listen.'

'So am I .'

The messdeck began to clear. Price and Brewster went up together and stood peering into the fog and listening. But the only sounds were the rhythmic throbbing of the *Emma*'s engines and the crackle and crunch of the loose ice as she pushed on through it.

'Object green-four-oh!' shouted the bridge lookout.

While they were training their binoculars from the bridge Alastair sent up the next cry.

'It's a boat – a mon in a boat!'

The commands came from the bridge.

'Starboard twenty . . . Midships . . . Port ten . . .'

The steam whistle was sounded in short, single blasts and Signalman Garrett kept flashing his Aldis lamp to attract the attention of the man in the boat, who through chinks in the fog could be seen moving about. But he did not seem to heed the approaching trawler, he was too busy struggling to lift something over the side. As they watched, he successfully jettisoned the load.

'Slow-ahead . . . Stop engines . . . Half-astern . . . Port twenty . . .'

110

They stood ready with heaving lines, a grapnel on a rope, a boathook, blankets, and the first-aid chest.

In response to their cries the muffled figure caught one of the lines, attached it to the boat and waved. They began to haul the boat alongside.

'Hey, you guys,' he croaked – 'what kept ya?' And he laughed wheezily.

11

He was unmistakably American, straight out of all the Hollywood movies they had ever seen. He had a round, rugged face
and seemed of average build, but was buried deep in a
voluminous padded leather coat with a fur collar. Before being
helped on board he dug his hands under the coat and produced,
like a magician from a hat, fold after fold of chocolate coloured
blanket which he had stuffed all round his middle and over his
chest in order to keep warm.

Once on board he stood and gingerly tested his cramped legs,
brushing aside attempts to support him. He then did a knees
bend, straightened up and slapped both limbs heartily, stamped
his feet and chuckled.

'How do you feel, chum?'

'Great. Just great!'

'Here, get this down you.'

The American took the proffered mug, drank a few mouth-
fuls, pulled a wry face and seemed about to spit, then changed
his mind and swallowed hard, afterwards licking his lips to clear
away the unfamiliar taste.

'Say, what do you call this?'

'Rum – Navy rum.'

'Yeah?' He looked at it suspiciously. 'Would you have any
coffee?'

'Yes,' said Jerry Baxter, who served it to the Wardroom. 'I'll
get you some.'

Relieved, the American handed back the mug of rum, still
exploring his teeth with his tongue.

'What happened, mate?'

'Torpedoed, I guess. Never saw the Kraut that hit us.'

'What ship?'

'The S.S. *John Dyson II*.'

'Did she go down?'

'Like a stone. Got a cigarette?'

Eager hands produced a packet of Player's, and he extracted one and cupped his hands to accept a light. After the first long draw of smoke he removed the cigarette and ran his tongue round the second alien taste in his mouth. 'English, eh?' he said tentatively. He did not wish to appear too ungrateful.

'What about the other survivors?'

The American took another long pull on the cigarette, grimaced at the taste and, looking back across the foggy sea, jerked a thumb in a generally northward direction.

'She cracked wide open and slid down. We carried a heavy load of guns and tanks. A lot of men were killed in the double explosion – we were carrying a lot of munitions. I reckon now there's only me.'

He turned back to face his rescuers. 'Harrigan. Able-bodied Seaman Noble Harrigan, that's me. Say, you *are* British Navy, aren't you?'

'Yes, mate.'

'Jeez-hell, I thought I was going kinda crazy when you came along – you looked like you'd come fishing!'

'This is an armed trawler.'

'You don't say?'

'How long were you in the boat?'

'A night and a day, I guess.' He seemed to be in surprisingly good shape after his icy ordeal.

'Stand back!' ordered Sub-Lieutenant Sibley as he approached. 'Come with me, please.'

'Sure thing.' Harrigan followed the No. 2 cheerfully up to the bridge.

After a few minutes the *Lady Emma*'s engines were restarted and she resumed her former course. Obviously, after questioning Harrigan, McBride had decided it was hopeless to search around for other survivors, even supposing the *Emma* could afford the precious time. The need to catch the convoy was doubly urgent, for if there was still a killer U-boat lurking in the frozen depths the *Emma*, with her Asdic dome gone, had no means of detecting it. Nevertheless the ship remained very quiet as all eyes and ears strained for sight or sound of any other life in the shrouded sea.

After a meal and a short sleep Harrigan lay quite talkatively in a bunk found for him on the messdeck, smoking a black cigar from a tin he had retrieved thankfully from a pocket of his leather coat. His questioners were able to build up a picture of what had happened to him.

The *John Dyson II*, one of three American merchant ships in the convoy, was a 'Liberty' ship of welded construction. When torpedoed – 'ripped open like a tin can' – and on the explosion of her ammunition she had simply burst apart and gone down in a very few minutes. She had been steaming at the rear of the convoy and, because of the fog and some steering trouble, had gradually lost distance. Harrigan was on deck portside when the double blast came. Shaken by the first blast he was hurled overboard by the second explosion and, in spite of his lifejacket, was near to drowning in his heavy clothes and with the shock of plunging into the freezing cold water, when he found a small boat which had been spewed out from the ship completely undamaged. He struggled into the boat, broke out its blankets from the emergency locker, sopped the seawater off himself with one of them and stuffed himself all over with the others. He heard faint voices away in the fog, but discovered that the boat was without oars, so he could only huddle there, drifting and listening. The voices died away until he was entirely alone. After some time he drifted close to a floating piece of timber on which a fellow seaman, barely alive, was straddled. With difficulty he pulled the man into the boat and wrapped him in blankets, but he was very badly injured and died shortly before the *Lady Emma* appeared out of the fog.

The questioners looked puzzled: Harrigan had been alone in the boat when they found him. Then some remembered the glimpse of him dumping something into the water just before his rescue. The thought of what that bundle had been was disturbing.

Harrigan saw the look in their eyes. 'He was dead. I said a Hail Mary before I put him over. He was Roman Catholic – ya know?'

No one spoke.

'His name was Dan Rogers, but we knew him as Texas Jack. Didn't owe a cent to any man, did Texas, and he had a kind word for everyone. God rest him.'

'Why did you put him over when you saw us coming?'

'Heck, pal, I didn't know whether you were Krauts or English

114

or Russkies or Eskimos! Anyhow, you didn't want to be bothered with burying him, did you?'

Big Ginger began to laugh, a high, nervous, gurgling laugh.

'What's so funny, fella?'

'Nothing, Yank,' said Eddie Nash. 'Forget it.'

'Are you really British Navy? You sure don't look it.'

'We're Patrol Service,' said Ted Beckles.

'What the heck's that? What patrol?'

'We're a convoy escort ship,' Beckles explained patiently.

'Yeah? Well, patrolman, as soon as I'm on my legs you tell me what I can do – I'll earn what I eat.'

'You'll have to see the Buffer.'

'The what?'

They drifted away, leaving Beckles to do all the explaining. Later, further scraps of information about Harrigan filtered their way around the crew. He was tough and tattooed. He had been a liquor-runner in the days of Prohibition. He described desperate encounters between the runners and the coastguard cutters, with machine-guns firing – this war business was nothing new to him. Had this 'boat' got machine-guns? Then he'd be glad of the chance to get back at those goddamned Square-heads ...

On the bridge Lieutenant Hadley, who had been hunched over the chart table pencilling a series of calculations, described his findings to the weary McBride.

'Allowing for between twenty to thirty degrees deviation of the magnetic compass, this would account for our rough passage in the ice,' said Hadley. 'The convoy, on the other hand, may have adjusted its course according to the gyro compass of the senior escort. It all adds up.'

McBride rubbed his darkened chin thoughtfully.

'In addition,' Hadley continued, 'I am not satisfied that in fixing the convoy's route the Admiralty planners allowed for the low position of the ice barrier at this time of year. In my opinion they routed us too far north, too close to the barrier. That seems to have been the cause of our trouble from the start.'

'Aye, that may be so.'

'By my calculations we have now steamed through Position Y. We have no further point of rendezvous until here, in the Barents Sea.' Hadley jabbed his finger at the chart. 'But if we take this new course, avoiding the ice as far as possible and making a steady eight knots, we should intercept them here.'

McBride nodded, got up from his chair and looked through the bridge window at the fog.

'With the wireless still under repair we cannot receive Admiralty signals,' Hadley added. 'Mr Grant cannot give us any guarantee that the repairs will be successful. And of course, with the failure of the Asdic we are now vulnerable to underwater attack.'

McBride gave him a weak smile.

'It couldna be much worse, Mr Hadley, could it now?'

'The *Lady Emma* is still an effective fighting ship, sir.'

'Aye, so she is, so she is.' McBride took up his binoculars. 'When this fog lifts, Number One, we will take your new course.'

On deck, Price was joined by Brewster.

'How's our survivor?'

'Oh, still talking away,' said Brewster. 'But he's got a partly frozen foot. Mr Grant has been working on it.'

'Harrigan is a real tough nut.'

'He says he sat in the boat singing and heaping curses on all the mean people he'd met in his life. That way he kept wide awake.'

'He's a walking miracle.'

They fell silent, staring out at the fog, both men wondering what their own reaction would have been if stranded alone in a boat in the dreadful Arctic night. On hearing a sharp cough Price glanced back and saw a figure climbing the ladder to the bridge verandah.

'There goes the Chief – off to see the Old Man again.'

Chief Hook entered the bridge through its single rear door. Scornful of the cold above decks he stood in his dirty, stained old Petty Officer's uniform with a sweat rag tied round his neck and an oily rag in his hand. His P.O.'s cap, slapped on to his greying head as a concessionary mark of respect, sat at a defiant angle.

'Well, Chief?' said McBride.

In hoarse tones Hook rasped, 'I've got trouble. One of my bearings is overheating – I'll have to stop engines and replace it.'

'How long will that take, Chief?'

' 'Bout a couple of hours or thereabouts.'

'Must it be done now?' said Hadley. 'Is there no other way – can't you just give it more oil?'

'I've tried extra fooking oil. I'll have to stop, I tell you.'

McBride pointed out at the fog. 'If we stop, Chief, we'll be

116

drifting blind. Can ye not fix it till we get a break in the weather?'

Hook shook his head firmly. 'We stop now, or else.'

'Very well, Chief, we'll just have to sweat it out.'

In a very short time the rhythmic beat of the *Lady Emma*'s engines died away and the clank of hammers and spanners was heard from the depths of the trawler as she wallowed in the fog.

'Double the lookouts, Mr Hadley,' McBride ordered.

'Aye, aye, sir.'

After about an hour, with the ship lying eerily still, it was noticed that the fog was beginning to thin out a little, but only, quirkily, on the starboard side to seaward, and then to some extent for'ard and aft. The resulting misty scene revealed the trawler to be ringed about by a mass of ice, great packed floes with scarcely a channel of water to be seen between them, while on the port side the fog remained thick, impenetrable and almost solid, like a towering escarpment. But behind it they could smell more ice – stretching, they needed no telling, in desolate, cavernous icefields away to the north. The *Emma* floated idly on the misty, circular expanse of enclosed water like a toy ship adrift in a children's boating pool.

'How do we get out of this bloody lot?' said Jack Barrow. 'If we don't start up soon we'll be hemmed in and frozen fast.'

Wally Winters studied the daunting ring of ice. 'There's a lot of hard ice,' he said, 'and some nasty looking bergs. But it will change, it's always changing. We'll find a way through once we start moving.'

'What an optimist. I bet you used to see fish where there wasn't any.'

On the port side, Price and James studied the great wall of fog.

'Out there be dragons,' James commented, 'with great green icebergs for teeth. And fog giants, and ice demons. I couldn't paint a better backdrop for a frozen opera.'

'It looks so solid,' said Price. 'It *is* fog, I suppose?'

'Yes, dear boy, that's all it is. You stick to your Seamanship Manual and leave the imaginative bits to me. At King Alfred you'll be able to tell the sprogs what an Arctic fog really looks like. Let's go starboard and take a look at that ice.'

On the bridge Bob Garrett, whose thoughts had been wandering, gave a sudden start, rubbed his frost-rimmed eyes and peered again into the fog bank. But what had attracted his attention was not, as he had first supposed, a trick of the light – it was the definite flicker of a lamp. At the same moment the portside lookout also saw it and let out a yell, 'Lamp flashing amidships!'

McBride was on his feet immediately as Garrett strained his eyes to read the flashing light issuing with some distortion from the fog. He read out the morse letters, one by one.

'W-h-a-t s-h-i-p-.'

McBride sighed with heavy relief and looked triumphantly at Hadley.

'Send them our call-sign, signalman!'

Garrett sent the call-sign and after an interval repeated it. When the mystery lamp flashed its next message out of the fog he again, with some difficulty, read it letter by letter, his companion signalman, Boone, having arrived to take down the message on his pad. When Garrett had finished, Boone stood clutching the pad, re-reading the wording as if mesmerised.

'Gi' it to me, mon!' McBride relapsed into his broad mother tongue as he eagerly took the pad, ripped off the signal paper and thrust the pad roughly back into Boone's stomach. But on reading the signal his exuberance melted away and he stood thunderstruck.

'What is it, sir?'

McBride passed the signal paper to Hadley. It read, 'You – are – in – my – sights – do – not – man – your – guns – do – not – start – engines – await – my – next – signal.'

'What the hell are they playing at?' Hadley demanded. 'Signalman, send "Who are you?" '

'Aye, aye, sir.' Garrett clicked out the question on his Aldis lamp. They waited for the answering signal.

'Do – not – man – guns – do – not – start – engines – you – are – warned.'

McBride read the message out aloud and turned to Hadley. 'What d'ye make of it?'

'Some blithering idiot doesn't recognise us. This fog plays tricks – to a merchant captain we could look like . . . like anything.'

'But evidently he can see our gun.'

'Yes,' Hadley agreed.

McBride blew the whistle of the voicepipe, snapped the lid open and said to the answering voice at the other end, 'How long now, Chief?'

'Half an hour, if you're lucky.'

'Right ye are.' McBride turned to Hadley. 'We canna move. We'll wait his next signal.'

'This blasted fog!' Hadley looked grimly at the dirty grey vaporous mountain that blocked their view. Then he frowned thoughtfully. 'That lamp, signalman. Did it seem to you to come from bridge height?'

'Hard to tell, sir. But it did seem a bit low down.'

'Flashing from a deck?'

'Could be, sir.'

Hadley raked the spot with his binoculars, but could see only the faint shapes of towering ice. Then the lamp began to flicker again.

'This – is – U 239 – one – false – move – you – will – be – torpedoed – stand – fast – await – instruction.'

'Germans!' McBride's hand went out to the alarm button, but stopped short.

'We're a sitting duck,' said Hadley.

'Aye.'

They waited tensely. The lamp began to flicker again.

'I – am – held – in – ice – you – will – break – me – out – with – your – bows – I – have – John – Dyson – survivors – they – will – be – handed – over – to – you – on – release – reply – now.'

As the full significance of the message dawned on both men McBride galvanised into action.

'Garrett, send "Have engine trouble, am repairing, give names of survivors." Number One, have Sibley and Grant report to the bridge. Can the American walk? I want him here too.'

Harrigan, hopping spryly and making light of his foot trouble, arrived with Sub-Lieutenant Grant just as the next reply had been received from the U-boat.

'Seaman Harrigan,' said McBride, signal paper in hand, 'do ye recognise these names – Ross, Carney, Adam, Wessell?'

Harrigan, for once at a loss for words, stood with his mouth open.

'Answer man,' said Hadley impatiently.

'Captain Ross – sure, my captain. Second Mate Abe Carney, Seaman Joe Adam, Rocky Wessell, engineer officer. Say, captain, what is this?'

'Could these men have survived when your ship was sunk?'

'Captain Ross was on the bridge when it blew. I saw it go,' said Harrigan, baffled.

'Let me put it another way – do ye know for a fact that these men could *not* have survived?'

'Waal, no, sir, I guess not.'

119

McBride nodded. There was always the suspicion that the U-boat had picked up the names from the ship's crew list, from wreckage or bodies found floating in the sea. When the *Emma*'s bridge had been cleared and he was alone with his three officers he marshalled the facts and declared his intentions. The tiredness had dropped from his face and he was alert and resolute.

The German commander's situation, he said, seemed clear. The U-boat, possibly deceived by the ice, had somehow become trapped. Obviously, to allow it to communicate by signal lamp, the greater part of the submarine must be on the surface. In the absence of any drift the trawler stood little chance against a 'fan' of torpedoes, the short distance between the two vessels allowing her little time to manoeuvre, additionally hampered as she was by the ring of ice. In these circumstances, to attempt evasive action immediately the engines restarted would be putting the ship and the lives of fifty men at high risk, for they could have no doubt that the German would carry out his threat – he was in a desperate position and had nothing to lose.

If, as demanded, they went to the U-boat's assistance, then during the time the *Emma* was pitting her weight against the ice there would probably be a 'blind' moment for the U-boat when they could attempt to spring a surprise and bring the trawler's guns to bear on it, but this depended on the guns being capable of the low angle and the position of the U-boat in the ice, and might prove difficult. At such close quarters they could not use depth-charges. There was also the consideration of the American captain and the other survivors, whom the German was using as 'insurance' and offering to barter in return for the release of his craft.

But if, on the other hand, they quite simply complied to the letter with the German's request and released, or sought to release, the U-boat they could expect immediately afterwards to be in a strong position to see that the German commander fulfilled his part of the bargain.

'And if he does not?' asked Hadley.

'As ye said earlier, Number One, this is a fighting ship.'

'Suppose we can't release the U-boat, sir?' said Grant.

'Then, laddie, we'll be safely out of his sights and in a position to call the next move.'

The voicepipe shrilled. 'Ready with engines.'

'Good work, Chief. Stand by.'

McBride quickly and with complete assurance dictated a final brief reply to the U-boat, and gave his officers their orders.

12

'Slow-ahead ... Wheel amidships ... '

Gently the *Lady Emma* moved forward, pushing light mush-ice away from her bows. Looming up starkly before them was the great wall of fog which blanketed out everything except the winking, guiding light from the U-boat.

As they crept nearer to the 'cliff face' a damp, muffling grey curtain descended uncannily over the trawler from bows to stern until they were right inside the dense foggy mass and could just glimpse a fantastic barrier of enshrouded ice rising in grotesque, jagged shapes from the murky surface of the sea. All hands had been ordered to be ready for instant action but not to man the guns until the Skipper gave the command. From their hiding places they strained their eyes to detect the first outline of the U-boat; trapped it might be, but the very thought of coming upon one of the dreaded 'wolves' of the sea at such close quarters made hearts beat faster.

'There he is!' yelled one of the bridge lookouts, pointing excitedly into the fog. 'There's Jerry – dead ahead!'

A dim, dark object was hazily visible below the winking light. McBride scanned it unsuccessfully through his binoculars and abandoned them for easier, quicker judgement with the naked eye. He could distinguish the shape of the conning tower, with a figure at the signal lamp, but see little of the hull, which appeared to be enclosed in a giant sandwich of jagged blue-green ice wreathed by the mist. He spoke calmly down the voice-pipe. 'Stop engines . . . Port twenty. Report how her head is every thirty seconds.' Through the opened window of the bridge

121

he ordered the lookouts, 'Report any movement from the U-boat instantly.'

Sibley and Grant were both at their stations on deck, ready to take charge of emergency manning of the guns and depth-charges. Hadley remained on the bridge beside McBride, having armed himself with his revolver and also placed a rifle within easy reach.

Suddenly the light stopped flashing and the figure on the conning tower was no longer visible. The *Emma*'s lookouts yelled the news.

'They've closed the hatch,' McBride told Hadley quietly. 'I'm going to push the ice on the starboard side.' He spoke into the voicepipe. 'Slow-ahead . . . Starboard ten . . . Half-ahead . . . Midships . . . Steady as ye go . . . Full-ahead . . .'

Steadily the *Lady Emma* gathered speed as she approached the ice packed around the U-boat and at six knots she struck with a reverberating crash that brought her to a quivering standstill.

'Emergency full-ahead . . . Hard-a-port . . .'

The *Emma*'s screw threshed the sea, spewing away loose ice like a mixer in a bowl and raising a plume of spray over the stern, while her bow ground against the obstruction and the whole ship vibrated and rattled like a bulldozer struggling to bite on stubbornly resisting rocks.

The engineroom pipe whistled shrilly and the Chief's voice rasped, 'You'll have to give over, Skipper – or you'll wreck my fooking engines.'

'Hang on, Chief, I think something's beginning to move.'

'My fooking bowels will, Mac, if you don't give oop soon . . .'

There was a tremendous crack as the seemingly solid sheet of ice suddenly gave way and split up like a pane of glass hit by a stone. The waters that were imprisoned below now came through it bubbling and splashing, swirling and spreading in all directions, angrily flinging out great agitated chunks of ice. The *Emma*'s bow cut into the splintered mass, pushing it all to one side, most of it away from the U-boat but some right up against its hull, which must have rocked its German crew.

In the thick, unyielding fog, with the great gurgle and swirl of disturbed water and ice, there was no indication of what had imprisoned the U-boat. It could have been caught by the ice anywhere, but more probably around its stern, under a shelf of the ice. The German commander had taken a double risk in seeking his craft's release in this desperate manner, for not only had he to rely on his enemy's word and the accurate manoeuvring of the trawler, but there was also the threat of serious damage to his craft, which might already have been maimed by the obstructing ice. But, with the conning tower above water, presumably he had had opportunity to size up his chances.

Slowly the great ice sandwich parted, bringing more of the U-boat into view. When trapped, its nose had been high up and its tail hidden, but now the after end rose above the surface and the nose went down, like the motion of a gigantic seesaw. It remained there upended and poised under a spray of fine mist, and the watching eyes on the trawler waited for it to level off and settle back on the surface of the ice strewn sea. But, oddly, it stayed where it was, as if suspended by invisible strings. It was a large craft, and though at that moment apparently helpless, it exuded an air of menace and imminent danger. To see it so close at hand was to understand and feel the fear that these raiders spread – the terror and the panic of hapless merchantmen.

They waited for the conning tower to open – any sign of life – but what happened next was entirely unexpected.

'The bastard's going!' yelled Jack Barrow on lookout.

Whether by intent or simply unable to help itself, the U-boat sank at an angle beneath the surface with a flurry of froth and bubbles, the uneasy loose ice immediately rushing back again to cover the spot where it had vanished and obliterate all trace.

'Stop engines . . . Slow-astern . . . Half-astern . . . Wheel amid-ships!'

After an agonising pause the *Lady Emma* came gradually astern and every man breathed a sigh of relief, for it would have been all too easy for the trawler to have followed the misfortune of the U-boat and become trapped herself in the hungry ice.

'Stop engines! All hands keep a good lookout and watch for wreckage.'

McBride searched the mist shrouded area where the U-boat had disappeared. Had it been holed by the pressure and sunk? If so, the end to the drama had come about in the simplest possible way.

'I don't like it,' said Hadley. He was becoming increasingly suspicious. Although he had accepted McBride's decision, he had not been too happy about the plan from the start. He would have preferred to attack the U-boat when the *Emma* had regained the power of her engines – to risk the torpedoes and

123

call the Germans' bluff. He was not a professional mariner like McBride and to him ships, whether British or enemy, were not living vessels or moving islands of souls, but purely instruments of the fight and nothing more. The thought of what might have happened to the *Emma* and her company had she been torpedoed did not enter into his reckoning – and certainly not the plight of the Germans. Now he was sure they should have attacked and destroyed the trapped U-boat – if the positions had been reversed, wouldn't the German have done the same to them? There was little that was chivalrous about those U-boat commanders who had cruelly machine-gunned British seamen as they took to their boats or swam for their lives in the sea.

The *Lady Emma* drifted and swung about aimlessly at the edge of the fog curtain, McBride being reluctant to move off and expose the trawler in the open without some evidence as to the fate of the U-boat.

'Object red-five-oh!'

All eyes turned in that direction to see first the periscope, then the conning tower, then the rounded shape of the U-boat rise from the depths like a great grey whale coming up to blow, shedding from its body streams of water and loose ice. It surfaced almost in the centre of the clear expanse of sea ringed with ice. The conning tower hatch was pushed open and men leapt out and ran furiously to the gun up for'ard.

'So that's his game,' grunted McBride. He pressed the alarm button. 'Action-stations!'

From all points of cover men in tin hats and lifejackets sprang into life and to their weapons, sliding and slipping about the *Emma*'s frozen deck.

'It's like Harringay bloody ice-rink at opening time!' gasped Eddie Nash to Price as thumps and bangs indicated that some men were taking tumbles. The four-inch crew tore across the well-deck and slithered up the icy steps of the ladder to the gun. In seconds the gun was cleared away, a shell and cartridge rammed into the breech, and 'Guns' was swinging the barrel over open sights on to the target. Within two minutes of reaching the platform they were ready to fire.

'On target,' shouted Grant to the bridge.

'Open fire,' bellowed McBride – 'and keep firing till ye hit the bastard!'

There was a burst of flame and a concussion which left the ears singing, and the stench of cordite filled the air. The range

124

was close and 'Guns' had to depress the barrel of the gun to its lowest limit, yet the shell whistled just over the heads of the German gunners, who seemed to be having trouble with their weapon. Seeing the difficulty in getting the *Emma*'s guns to bear McBride at once gave the order 'Full-astern!'

On the U-boat's conning tower a quick-firing gun opened up with tracers and cannon-shells which exploded with a vicious crack on the *Emma*'s hull, peppered deck fittings, raked one side of the bridge and struck the shield behind which the four-inch crew sheltered. Other shells zinged through the air just above deck level, uncomfortably close to the men upon it.

On the starboard side Hotchkiss, Sam the fisherman poured a stream of fire against the men on the conning tower, and for once his weapon was not jamming but firing in steady bursts. As McBride manoeuvred the *Emma*, going astern, he enabled the twin point-five to come into action and give heavier support to the lone Hotchkiss.

The four-inch continued to fire high-explosives at ten-second intervals but still the angle was too acute and this, combined with the faulty trigger, sent the shells hitting the sea just beyond the U-boat, sending up fountains of angry icy water over the German gun crew, who were still struggling to bring their main gun into action.

There was a sudden cry at the *Emma*'s four-inch and McDougal, who had been loading, spun round and collapsed on the platform, writhing and clutching at his left shoulder which had been hit by a glancing shell. Another man swiftly took his place while Tommy Tilson and Ernie Michael pulled the casualty across into cover.

Another burst of cannon-fire from the U-boat punctured a steampipe, sending clouds of steam hissing and flying about the *Emma*'s deck, obscuring the vision of gunners and lookouts. In the thick of it stoker Paddy Kelly dashed up and, coolly ignoring the firing and the hot steam, began to patch the shrieking hole by wrapping a thick layer of asbestos sheeting round it.

All at once the German gunners were seen to abandon their struggles with the U-boat's big gun and start running back to the conning tower.

'They've had enough!' cried Hadley.

McBride shook his head. 'We'll have to be quick – he's going to dive.' He weighed up the situation rapidly. The question was, could the trawler's four-inch strike the target before the U-boat dived? And if not, could he make a depth-charge attack? He was going full astern but it would take time to get much way on, and to drop depth-charges at a shallow setting would mean getting up to full-ahead to avoid having the *Emma*'s stern blown off, which seemed impossible in the prevailing conditions.

In seconds he had made up his mind and was rapping out a quick succession of orders. 'Stop engines . . . Slow-ahead . . . Half-ahead . . . Full-ahead . . . Emergency full-ahead . . . Port ten . . . Midships . . . Starboard ten . . . Midships . . . Steady as ye go . . . '

It took time to come from full-astern to full-ahead and McBride feared he was going to be too late, but the U-boat, its conning tower now cleared and hatch closed, seemed very sluggish in making its dive, and he fervently hoped that it was having some trouble in doing so. As the trawler gathered speed he gave a stream of course corrections to Wally Winters on the wheel to keep the *Emma* dead on target – just forward of the conning tower, where he hoped to bite deep into the slowly moving U-boat. Scattering loose ice before her the *Emma* cleft the sea like a knife – and still the U-boat strangely did not submerge – clearly it had been damaged in the ice and was not responding properly to the controls. Why, then, had the German commander persisted in his offensive action against such odds?

Now there was only a hundred yards to go, fifty, twenty – until with a jarring crash the trawler hit the U-boat's hull dead on line as it was settling below the surface of the water, and sank her sharp bow deep into it. Still with some way on her the *Emma* continued ahead, pushing the half-submerged U-boat before her like a dog with a bone.

The jolt had flung the *Emma*'s crew off their feet. The ship's bow could be seen to be buckled and crumpled, and the one thought uppermost after the impact was, had she holed herself below the waterline? They could see the sea pouring into the great rent in the U-boat's side, the increasing list it was taking, and it took little imagination to guess at the panic that must be ensuing within that grey hull, the screams, shouts and groans as men fought to escape.

McBride was giving orders again in calm tones. 'Stop engines . . . Slow-astern . . . Half-astern . . . '

The *Lady Emma*'s bows disentangled from the U-boat and withdrew slowly.

'Stop engines,' ordered McBride, and as the *Emma* continued to drift slowly astern the gaze of every man on deck was riveted on the awesome spectacle of a submarine in its death throes.

Now, surely, there would be some movement of men from the crazily leaning conning tower . . . but the U-boat gave a violent lurch, recovered momentarily, and then rolled right over to reveal its bottom. For seconds only it lay wallowing like a stricken porpoise, sinking ever lower in the water, then it disappeared amid a mass of oily bubbles.

There were no cheers, only a long, deep silence as the *Emma*'s crew stared at the spot where the German had gone down.

'It might have been oursen, tha knows,' said one of the Yorkies, airing the thoughts of many.

'Aye, there but for the grace of God . . . ' said Tommy Tilson.

On the bridge Lieutenant Hadley gazed with undisguised satisfaction at the now empty patch of sea. 'Congratulations, sir,' he said, and meant it wholeheartedly.

McBride passed a hand over his aching forehead and sighed. 'Poor divils,' he said slowly. 'Murdering Nazi bastards they may be – but what a way to go . . . Mr Hadley, inspect the damage for'ard.'

'Aye, aye, sir.'

A great pool of oil was spreading on the sea, broken by bursting bubbles and drifting ice-blocks. Then something more solid appeared – a big sheet of canvas, followed by small items of debris and a jumble of articles of clothing. After a time the *Emma*'s watchers saw, floating, a shapeless sack-like object; only it was not a sack, it was a human body. Then more were sighted, until Eddie Nash had counted seven of them.

On the bridge, where he had been joined by Sub-Lieutenant Grant, McBride turned his binoculars on to each of the bodies as they were buffeted about by the swell. Clearly there were no signs of life as they disappeared into and in some cases under a mass of loose ice.

'We could search the bodies for papers, sir,' Grant suggested.

McBride put down his binoculars. 'We could, Mr Grant,' he said grimly. 'But I will not put my ship back into that ice.'

Lieutenant Hadley returned to the bridge. 'The forepeak is crushed and full of water, but the after bulkhead is holding and I think it will stand up if we don't hit any more ice at speed.'

'Thank you, Number One.' McBride's craggy face relaxed into a tired smile. 'We will now proceed on your course to intercept the convoy.'

'Aye, aye, sir.'

'What was that?' said Grant suddenly.

He hurried out on to the bridge verandah to see the cause of new shouts from the deck, and returned to report. Alastair had spotted another body, well away from the ice, this time floating properly in its lifejacket.

'He swears he saw it wave or move an arm, sir.'

'He did?' McBride trained his binoculars on the man in the sea and, after a moment's deliberation, gave orders.

As the trawler came alongside the floating man, Price, Beckles and big Ginger lowered Barrow over the side on a rope. Barrow carried another line which he expertly secured around the survivor.

'I think he's still alive!' Barrow shouted up.

They hauled the two on board and laid the rescued man on the deck. Barrow, a blanket thrown round his shoulders, tried to rouse his charge, but there was no movement from him and the eyes in the drawn face were glazed. Sub-Lieutenant Grant got to his knees, took hold of a limp arm and felt the pulse, then struggled to get his hand through the man's clothing to his heart. When he found it he shook his head regretfully.

'We're too late. He's dead.'

Willie the Buffer knelt down and put his head close to the face of the body. 'Aye,' he said. 'He's gone.' Gently, with his thumb, he closed the eyelids over the sightless eyes.

'Any papers on him?' asked Sub-Lieutenant Sibley sharply.

Finding nothing in a breast pocket, Grant wrestled to free more of the man's clothing. Then he stopped and looked up at Sibley.

'This man is an officer, but not of the German Navy. I think he's wearing a merchant jacket.'

Sibley bent down and examined the jacket. At that moment the same thought occurred to both officers and Sibley straightened up and turned to Price. 'Fetch Seaman Harrigan.'

'Aye, aye, sir.'

Price found Harrigan on his bunk, morosely resting his leg. The American followed him protestingly up to the deck.

'Harrigan – can you identify this man?' Sibley asked.

For a moment Harrigan gazed dully at the body stretched out at his feet. Then he looked at Sibley, his eyes narrowed. 'Sure,' he said. 'That's Captain Ben Ross.'

Sibley departed for the bridge to take the news to McBride. Grant straightened the clothes on the body and stood up.

'I'm sorry, Harrigan.'

'Yeah,' said the American laconically. He turned and limped away down to the messdeck.

'Mr Grant!' called McBride from the bridge.

'Yes, sir?'

'Attend to the Captain.'

'Aye, aye, sir. Price, Meeson – get a stretcher.'

On the bridge, McBride gave orders for the *Lady Emma* to proceed on her way. He looked back thoughtfully at the receding ice and began to pace the bridge slowly with tired legs.

'We'll give Captain Ross a proper burial, Mr Hadley. Please make the arrangements.'

Later, under the whaleback, Willie Campbell and Alastair silently wrapped the dead officer in canvas sheeting with firebars at his feet, and sewed him up in his shroud using a 'palm and needle' to work the strong sailor's twine. This unsettling job done, an improvised canvas shute was rigged up and fastened to the ship's rail. When all was ready the Buffer scratched his head, consulted his store lists, and searched about in a cupboard. He eventually found what he sought and then went to Lieutenant Hadley to explain.

'As we've no American flag, sir, I've covered the Captain's body wi' a Union Jack. D'ye think the poor mon would mind?'

'No, Campbell,' said Hadley, his face expressionless. 'I'm sure he would not.'

The *Emma* stopped engines and all hands not on watch were mustered at the ship's side. Price watched the quiet scene from his position on lookout.

McBride read from a Prayer Book provided by the Buffer. 'Man that is born of a woman hath but a short time to live, and is full of misery. He cometh up, and is cut down, like a flower . . . he fleeth as it were a shadow, and never continueth in one stay. In the midst of life we are in death . . . of whom may we seek for succour, but of thee, O Lord.'

The *Lady Emma* lurched in the swell and they steadied themselves on their feet.

'Forasmuch as it hath pleased Almighty God of his great mercy to take unto himself the soul of our dear brother here departed, we therefore . . . ' – McBride turned the pages of the Prayer Book to the section for burial at sea, marked for him by the Buffer with a piece of cardboard – ' . . . commit his body to the deep, to be turned into corruption, looking for the resurrection of the body, when the sea shall give up her dead, and the life of the world to come, through our Lord Jesus Christ, who at his coming shall change our vile body, that it may be like his glorious body, according to the mighty working, whereby he is able to subdue all things to himself.'

He signalled, and the men holding the deck end of the canvas shute raised it, sending the body sliding down into the sea with a sombre splash.

'The grace of our Lord Jesus Christ, and the love of God, and the fellowship of the Holy Ghost, be with us all evermore.'

'Amen,' murmured the assembled company.

'Caps on,' ordered Sibley.

McBride handed back the Prayer Book to the Buffer, walked off and climbed to the bridge.

'Slow-ahead . . . '

As the ship began to move again Price glanced back at the now distant ice and its darkly shrouding fog banks. They were steering a more southerly course now, away from the grim wastes which had claimed so many lives. McBride's brief service, he knew, had been held not only for Captain Ross but for all those other lives, American and German, lost in the *John Dyson* and the U-boat. For the sea knew no differences between men.

For the rest of his time on lookout Price scanned the ever clearing sea. When would they see another friendly ship?

'Watch-o, mate – wakey, wakey!'

It was Tommy Tilson, his relief. He handed over his lookout position and started for the wheelhouse to take over the wheel from Ted Beckles, on the way exploring with his fingers lines of small, jagged holes made by the enemy cannon-shells. They had survived, and sunk a U-boat, but because of all else that had happened the enormity of their success had not yet fully registered. The routine of the ship would go on as before. Already, he learned, big Ginger was taking bets on how long it would take them to catch up with the convoy in the Barents Sea.

13

Eddie Nash had been listening with curling lip to the expressions of two Yorkie stokers, whose conversation was littered with 'thees' and 'thous' and 'thys' and 'theesens'; to hear them was like listening to a dialect play on the wireless. It was too much for the little Londoner, who leapt up and stood belligerently, feet firmly planted, as he might on board his Thames barge.

'Well,' he said, thrusting his jaw out pugnaciously at one of the stokers, 'have you done *owt*? Or will there be *nowt* doing *while* tomorrow? Why the hell you bleedin' Yorkies can't speak proper I just don't know!'

'We speak better'n you ignorant Cockneys, tha knows.'

'Better than us? That's a laugh. It's King's English what *we* speak.'

'If King spoke like thee, lad, he'd soon get bloody sack.'

'Why, you bleedin' pudden-bashers, you're as bad as the Scots, who *are* foreigners, anyway.'

'Will you be telling that to the Old Man, then, Eddie?' inquired another stoker.

'Aw, go poke your bleedin' fires.' He stumped across the mess-deck and flung himself on his bunk.

'Temper, temper,' said James mildly.

'As for you, Lord Muck . . .'

Nash was interrupted as McDougal came slowly down the ladder, his arm in a sling.

'It's our honourable casualty,' said James warmly. 'Had your dressing changed, Doog?'

McDougal nodded miserably. Not even the new glow of comradeship radiated to him by everyone as a result of his

131

wound could lessen the permanent gloom in which he lived, breathed and slept.

'Cheer up, lad, you've only lost a bit of flesh,' said Jack Barrow. 'You'll soon make it up. Lucky it didn't hit the bloody bone.'

'I think he should get a medal,' said Nash generously, his irritation forgotten.

'Aye. Pinned on by Cross-Buckets,' said Sam.

'The Old Man's sure to get a medal,' said Barrow. 'I bet it'll be a D.S.O.'

'They ought to pin something on the *Emma*,' said Wally Winters quietly. 'She deserves it right enough.'

His remark spurred a quick interest from those seated by the fire.

'Aye – what a battering the old tub took. We're bound to go for a refit now.'

'What – in Russia? What's the bloody good of that?'

'No, it'll be G.Y. when we get back – a long refit, and lots of lovely leave.'

'Seeing as we've bleedin' earned it.'

'The *Emma* will be famous – actually sinking a U-boat! They'll be as jealous as hell in the *Crystal*.'

'We'll all be heroes, lads.'

'Aye, it'll be on the wireless – they'll have the flags out when we get home.'

'*If* we get yam,' growled Geordie.

'Course we will, lad – now we're out of yon bloody ice.'

That night the card school was restarted in the after mess, a familiar, reassuring sight from Northern Patrol days which confirmed that all was well as the *Lady Emma* rode at good speed through a sea only thinly scattered with harmless small ice. The gamblers played in good heart at the mess table, big mugs of tea at their elbows. As usual the pack was carefully shuffled and given to Ginger, who with great deliberation dealt them out, and as during the game the cards fell steadily they were scooped up in his great fist. He was the king, bland and scheming; Eddie Nash played his cards briskly, keen as a knife; Geordie clung to his, grim and suspicious; Tommy Tilson hummed a tuneless air.

'For Christ's sake, why didn't you play your queen?' demanded Jack Barrow threateningly of Sid the stoker. Ginger sighed and soothed them both with a gentle wave of his mutton fingers.

'You know your trouble, lad,' he said, addressing the stoker like a tutor correcting his stumbling pupil, 'you can't count. If you can't count up here' – he stabbed his forehead with a horny thumb – 'then do it on your fingers . . . only don't let me *see* you doing it.'

As the game continued, Eric Brewster found himself steadily winning, and became increasingly embarrassed by the riches which were pushed across to him. Ginger eyed him benevolently as they finished.

'How much have you got there, son?'

'Nearly three quid,' said Brewster, blushing. 'I . . . er . . . '

Ginger got up from the table and slapped him heartily on the back.

'Don't you fret – I'll win it all back from you tomorrow!'

And everyone knew that he would.

A night spell on the wheel, steering the ship by the bright dial of the compass which swung before and above him, could have a hypnotic effect on a man after a time. Price, doing his best to keep a clear head, was relieved when James entered the wheelhouse, shrugging the cold from his shoulders, and breezily broke the monotony.

'Yankee Doodle,' said James, 'has found his voice again.'

'Oh?' said Price apprehensively. 'He's not criticising the Old Man?'

James laughed, waving away the suggestion that Harrigan blamed the Skipper for the deaths of his fellow Americans in the U-boat.

'No, no hard feelings – nothing like that. Our tough friend is a realist – he's waxing on about something more dear to his soul. Liberty ships.' He adopted a nasal twang. ' "Those goddamned tin cans! Jeez-hell, I'd sooner sign on in a Hog Islander any day. In those Liberties you only wanna powerboat to go passing by and you start rolling. Great waddling bastards! Heck, they can't even stand up in a storm – I heard of one Liberty that broke into three lousy pieces and it didn't need the help of no Kraut torpedo, no sir!" '

'Are they really as bad as that?' asked Price.

'Who knows?' James shrugged. 'I know they're all-welded ships, pushed out at speed by the American shipyards – so they sound a bit dodgy. According to Harrigan the *John Dyson* was doomed anyway, she was such an unwieldy vessel. But there's something else that's really bothering him – makes him quite fierce.'

'What's that?'

'He's unemployed – official. Seems that the minute the ship went down he went off the company's payroll. He says the moment he left the ship his wages automatically stopped – it's the law in the American merchant service.'

'But he didn't leave his ship – the ship left *him*.'

'Exactly. That's why he's so mad. And don't say, "Don't they know there's a war on?" . . . '

The door opened and Bob Garrett looked in.

'How long, Bob?' asked James.

The signalman pursed his lips and eyed them both. 'About thirty to thirty-six hours. But I haven't told you.'

'I'll get your kye,' said James approvingly. 'And I'll see it's hot.'

It was mid-morning on a grey, forlorn but ice-free sea, with the *Lady Emma*'s engines throbbing comfortably as she forged ahead, when Jack Barrow ran for'ard and stumbled down the messdeck ladder.

'Cross-Buckets has gone bloody mad – gave me a hell of a bollocking. He says a depth-charge key's missing. Ted, Eddie, Ginger – what do you know about that?'

The three others who, with Barrow, comprised the depth-charge party looked at each other mystified.

'What key?' echoed Beckles.

'The one from the charge we exploded before going to Iceland. If any of you know anything about it you'd better get down there, by Christ!'

But all three men shook their heads. They were still trying to make sense of Barrow's news when the call came from the hatch.

'Beckles! Meeson! Report to Sub-Lieutenant Sibley at the depth-charge station forthwith!'

They went off muttering, leaving Eddie Nash still puzzling and wondering why he had not been summoned too. But when, minutes later, the call came for him, he suddenly knew why. Sibley had deliberately questioned the others first, and eliminated them, in order to steer the blame in one certain direction.

He found Sibley standing alone close to the depth-charge throwers. The officer's face was tightly drawn, and when he spoke it was with a conscious effort to keep his voice cool and firmly under control.

'Nash, Number Three depth-setting key is missing. Who last had Number Three key?'

Nash thought quickly. The depth-setting key for each depth-charge was in the detonator tube which was pushed into the depth-charge before firing, and it automatically sprang out when a setting had been put on the dial; all keys had to be kept and later turned in ashore to account for depth-charges used. It would have been an instinctive action for him to retrieve the key and place it on a hook on the rack to be collected by Sibley in the normal way. Now he tried desperately to recall the incident, but his mind remained a blank.

'Number Three key was your responsibility – isn't that so?'

Sibley knew very well that it was, his grilling of the other three men would have established the fact. Nash walked across to the rack. The protecting bar was in its place across the hooks, but number three hook was empty.

'Now think carefully, Nash – what did you do with the key?'

'I put it on the hook after firing.'

'But it is not there, Nash.'

Nash looked vainly round the deck.

'Maybe it fell off when we hit the ice.'

'But the bar is in place.'

'Perhaps the bar became loose – and was locked back by someone afterwards. Or the cannon-shells from the U-boat dislodged it.'

'I have examined the area. No bullets or shells struck this part of the ship.'

'Well, I did hang the key up,' said Nash defiantly.

'But it is not there.'

It was becoming increasingly more difficult for Sibley to contain himself, but he continued to choose his words carefully as they came thinly from his tight-lipped mouth. 'Nash, this is a very serious loss. As you are aware, every key has to be accounted for. As the officer in charge I am held responsible – it is my *personal* responsibility. I must bring such a loss to the notice of the Commanding Officer and also put in a full report to the N.O.I.C. Now think, Nash – *what did you do with the key?*'

Nash sensed the growing menace behind Sibley's statement. It was usual for the officer in charge to collect up the keys after firing and keep them in the Wardroom, but in the chaotic events of that night, when two of the depth-charges had refused to be rolled off and only the thrower had fired a single 'can', routine had gone by the board. By rights, if the key was now missing Sibley himself was half to blame – but he was thrusting it squarely on to his shoulders. He tried hard to recall the scene but still could not picture what he had done with the key. The No. 2 had him, like a winkle on a pin. But he would not squirm.

'I put the bleedin' thing on the hook. If it's gone I don't know where it is. You should have collected it.'

The light of elation came to Sibley's eyes.

'Nash, you will report to me in ten minutes, properly dressed, to appear before the Commanding Officer.'

'I'm fucked if I will!'

The Cockney's fists were clenched. Sibley took a pace forward, as if deliberately inviting retaliation. 'You won't get out of *this*, Nash,' he hissed. 'I'll see to it that you don't.'

Nash slowly began to raise an arm. It was the end. He was beyond caring. He wanted to hit, and hurt, that closely leering face. His fist was clenched so tightly that the fingernails bit deeply into his palm –

'Hello there!'

The bearded figure of Ernie Michael came strolling across the deck.

'What do you want?' snapped Sibley.

'I think I've got something belonging to you,' said Michael casually. He fished into his duffle coat and held up the object, dangling it between finger and thumb. 'Depth-charge key, isn't it?'

Sibley gazed at the key unbelievingly.

'Found it on deck after we'd rammed the U-boat – there was a bit of a mess. Forgot about it when carrying McDougal. Just remembered it.'

Sibley looked at him with face aflame and snatched the key from his hand. 'Why didn't you report this?'

'Well,' said Michael, unperturbed, 'there was a lot going on, wasn't there?'

Sibley looked hard into the face of the H.S.D. and read there nothing but insolent contempt.

'Do you take me for a complete bloody fool?' he said savagely.

Michael feigned a look of sheer innocent surprise. 'Me, *Mister* Sibley?'

The No. 2 turned back to Nash. 'Be more alert in future. *Smarten up*. Dismissed.'

He turned and strode away.

On the messdeck later big Ginger, when the scene was described to him by Michael, tittered and shook and guffawed and finally dissolved into great peals of shrill laughter, slapping his thighs with his huge hands, and the merriment spread from man to man until the whole of the messdeck was roaring. It was Ginger who, after returning from questioning by Sibley, had quickly gone round telling everyone of the plight of Eddie Nash, and in doing so had jogged Michael's memory. Only Nash, after appreciatively ruffling the big man's ginger thatch as he rolled about helplessly, was unable to join in the general amusement. He was shaken almost to breaking point. He had been only a whisker away from striking Sibley and the horror of a term shut up in cells.

'Don't brood, Eddie lad,' said Ted Beckles quietly. 'The man isn't worth it. Something tells me Cross-Buckets won't be with us much longer. He's a sick devil – in more ways than one.'

'Out of his bloody mind,' said Jack Barrow. 'And so were the silly bastards who made him an officer in the first place.'

'Aye,' added Sam, 'Remember how he used to sneak around the deck in his plimsolls, trying to catch us out on watch?'

'Yes – till Jimmy the One told him off.'

'And the lamp,' said Sam. 'Don't forget the lamp.'

As if they ever would. There were murmurs and nods of heads. The incident of *the lamp* was written deep into the *Lady Emma*'s history. When a lamp was found to be missing from the Wardroom while the ship was in harbour at Kirkwall, with both McBride and Hadley ashore, Sibley had conducted a full scale witch-hunt, questioning every man and threatening to stop all shore leave unless the culprit owned up. The messdeck held its own 'court of inquiry' and eventually the culprit confessed and was propelled to the Wardroom with the lamp he had 'borrowed' and neglected to return, and their leave was saved. So was the 'criminal', since drafted to another ship, who, on the timely intervention by Hadley, had been given suitable punishment instead of being marched off to Base and the cells by the vengeful Sibley.

'The man's a bloody maniac,' said Barrow. 'He ought to be ashore looking after the piss'oles – and that job's too good for him.'

In the afternoon the leaden grey sky became heavily overcast and patchy fog returned, though not dense enough to cause the *Lady Emma* to slacken speed. There was an air of determination now about her steady, uninterrupted progress and the resolute throbbing of her engines, which made it all the more of a shock when the alarm-bells clanged twice for an aircraft alert.

They tumbled out to the guns, shivering in the cold and searching everywhere in the overcast sky for a sign of the plane. Wally Winters, who had given the alarm, swore he had heard the drone of aircraft engines and now Alastair, listening with his head on one side, also claimed to hear it. Then the others heard it, the muffled drone of engines coming intermittently out of the fog, high above. The guns were readied.

'Is it one of ours?' asked one of the four-inch crew.

'What? Right out here in the Barents Sea? Some hopes!'

'Could be a Russian plane, come to see us in.'

'Mebbe.'

But no one was really inclined to believe that. They stayed silent as 'Guns' sought to trace the direction of the plane, already suspecting that its high, steady path was well out of their range, for the four-inch was never intended for use against aircraft and was essentially a surface gun; it could not elevate much more than forty-five degrees. Only at close quarters, against low-flying aircraft, did it have any chance of acquitting itself.

The drone gradually faded away, but, after an interval, returned. It grew steadily louder. They strained their ears to detect from which direction it was coming, but in the fog sound was highly deceptive. Then all at once the black shape of a seaplane loomed fleetingly out of the mist in the opposite direction from that in which they had trained the gun, hanging high in the sky like a giant dragon-fly. As they hurriedly swung the gun round the fog quickly masked it again, but not before Sub-Lieutenant Grant had confidently identified it.

'It's a Blohm-and-Voss – a long-range plane. Out on patrol by the looks of it.'

The droning receded after the plane had passed almost overhead, then became audible again as it circled, still out of sight, and came back on another path without altering height. Twice more they glimpsed its black shape through the fog, then the sound of its engines died away in the distance.

'Do you think it's seen us, sir?'

'I don't know,' said Grant, trying to appear more unconcerned than he really felt. Had the plane come searching not for them but for one of its own? Had the U-boat sent out wireless signals while trapped in the ice? It was a thought, and not a pleasant one, if in seeking the U-boat the plane should find them.

They remained at action-stations for an hour after the plane had gone. During the long vigil Price, at the four-inch, found himself thinking back to his early gunnery training. The instructors had had a language all their own and could teach only by constant use of the interrogative 'Or right?' The staccato words now ran idly through his head.

'When the bullet leaves the barrel – *or right?* – the gases escape through here – *or right?* – and take up against the piston – *or right?* – forcing it to the rear – *or right?* – thus bringing the breech-lock and moving parts to the rear – *or right?* – and then the sear – *or right?* – takes up against the cutaway portion – *or right? ...* '

He came out of his reverie to find 'Guns' flapping his arms round his chest for warmth as the baker man used to do at home when delivering on a freezing cold morning.

'The booger isn't coming back!'

'If he saw us he isn't interested – he's looking for ships, not an old fishing tub.'

'We're not worth a bloody bomb – and that's a fact!'

They stood down with relief, and the fortunate ones who were not on duty scuttled off smartly to thaw themselves out in front of the messdeck fire. There, hours later, the talk turned to Murmansk, or 'Murmanx' as some called the tongue-twisting Russian port for which they were heading. In particular, they discussed the girls they might hopefully see there.

'All those brawny women building roads and bridges and pulling tractors ... '

'They don't *pull* tractors.'

'Well then, driving 'em. I tell you they'll be muscle-bound anyway.'

'Come off it, mate, there's got to be some young bits of skirt.'

'Jerry will be looking out for *them*.'

Curly-haired Jerry Baxter smiled a smug smile. His chief hobby was collecting a suitcase full of chocolates and cigarettes to charm the girls back home with on his next leave. Now at least he could look forward to putting the contents of the suitcase to good use among the Russian 'talent'.

'How about Tom? He'll be chasing after the other women.'

Telegraphist Tom Knox, fluffy-haired but going bald, which gave him a Churchillian appearance, snorted. A former travelling salesman from Nottingham, he was used to all the nudging jokes about commercial travellers which were flung at him.

'Now if you had a bit of your Nottingham lace to whistle under their noses, Tom...'

'Wait till the Doog shows them his war wound – he'll soon have his feet under the table.'

McDougal, with his good hand, felt his trussed up shoulder and gave a thin, only half miserable smile.

'Hey,' called Harrigan from his bunk. 'Save one of those Russkie dames for me, fellas.'

'Sure, Yank.'

'And we'll have to chain Paddy down – there'll be a right shemozzle when he gets a taste of the vodka!'

The big stoker beamed and chuckled, basking in the limelight.

The banter continued as Knox left for the wireless cabin and was still in full swing when Shelley, the second telegraphist, came down from watch. The wireless was working again, but only in fits and starts, and as yet no signals had been picked up.

'Give us a tune, lad.'

Shelley needed no second invitation. Out came the ukulele and they were soon joining in 'I'm Leaning On A Lamp-Post'. They sang with an air of joyous relief and anticipation of the sight of the convoy and then Russia. In the middle of 'Bless 'em All' Boone, the weasel-faced signalman, suddenly got up and began to tap dance. He was good, very good, and they clapped and urged him on delightedly. When he gave up, exhausted, several men got up to dance together, and then Ginger's powerful voice launched into the popular ditty about painting the ship's side. A crescendo of other voices joined in the choruses – 'Sibley'll have a blue fit, if he sees any shit, on the side of the old *Lady Emma*!' As Ginger reached a hoarse peak of song so did the others. 'Roll on the *Rodney*, the *Nelson*, *Renown*, the bloody old *Emma* is getting me down!' Then they too fell back exhausted, and Ginger's singing tailed off into convulsive shrieks of laughter.

'Come on, "Guns",' came the shouts, 'let's have "Dirty Little Drawers!"'

The sturdy figure of 'Guns' rose from the throng with a gratified grin on his face. This was his party piece and he loved performing it. Waving his hairy arms about, he burst into a raucous and not very tuneful baritone. When he reached the chorus of 'The dirty little drawers that Maggie wore' everyone joined in with a roar that threatened to bring down the bulkheads. Verse after verse followed with 'Guns's' round face

140

getting redder and redder and his gestures ever more extravagant. At last the end came and he sat down to gusty cheers and applause with the satisfaction of one who had done his turn to the full. Shelley's ukulele started up again and more men got up to dance. Harrigan, who had watched with disbelief the spectacle of the first sailors dancing had now joined in the singing, his flat voice baying out lustily, his good foot stamping the deck with relish. The impromptu concert continued with a wild swing, all men hungry for more, until suddenly the voices and music faltered and stopped, and the dancers halted awkwardly in mid-dance. Sub-Lieutenant Grant had descended the messdeck ladder.

'I appreciate your high spirits, men, but could you please make a little less noise?'

They gaped at him, too keyed up to cope with the unexpected intrusion, but the Buffer was quick to respond and save the young officer's obvious embarrassment.

'Aye, aye, sir.'

Grant smiled apologetically and returned up the ladder. Only very rarely did a duty officer set foot on the messdeck except at prescribed times.

'That bastard Cross-Buckets sent him,' snarled Jack Barrow. 'Too bloody scurvy to come himself.'

They continued singing, a little less boisterously now, until another figure descended the ladder.

'Come on, James, give us some bloody Shakespeare. '

There were loud groans. 'Oh, not that!'

But James obligingly struck a pose and began to declaim. 'Friends, Romans, countrymen, lend me your ears, I come to bury Sibley, not to praise him, the evil that men do lives after them, the good is oft interred with their bones, so let it be with – '

He ducked against a hail of boots.

'Posh booger!'

'You long streak of diarrhoea,' James quickly countered. 'Verily,' he addressed them all, 'thou art na men, but dogs.' He crossed to Price's bunk. 'All's well,' he announced, 'the Old Man's left the bridge and is down in his cabin at last, sleeping like a baby. Have fun aloft.'

Price nodded and glanced up at Brewster, who was lying very quiet. Too quiet.

'What are you thinking about, Eric?'

Brewster's boyish face peered over the edge of the bunk,

sheepishly. 'Preston,' he said. 'I was wondering how they're doing.'

'Football? I thought you had other things on your mind.'

'Yes,' Brewster admitted, conscious of the letter which he had been re-reading for the umpteenth time, now stuffed under his pillow.

'They're not a bad team,' said Price.

'I wanted to be a footballer once.'

'I'll try you out,' Price offered. 'We'll organise a game – in Russia.'

The wind was keen and cold as he reached the deck, but the grey-black night sea was in temperate mood and there was no ice, nor any sign of it, only more patchy fog. Before ascending to the bridge he instinctively looked aft and was surprised to see a silent shape hunched at the ship's starboard side. It was Alastair. Above the collar of the Stornowegian's duffle coat Price saw his gauntly exposed head and the outline of his prominently boned face. He was sitting looking out to sea and at the sky, listening. The man should have been in his bunk. Was he ill, perhaps? He had lately been spitting more than usual.

For a moment Price hesitated, then he shrugged and continued on his way. During his watch he looked back and tried to see if Alastair was still there, but could not pick out his shadowy figure. Yet he was aware in an eerie kind of way that the quiet man had not moved and was still there, hunched and listening.

They were now within hours of sighting the convoy.

14

Dawn broke in a watery haze with banks of fog looming here and there like huge wads of dirty cotton wool dropped on to the surface of the sea. Ted Beckles contemplated the dank, dreary scene and spat over the ship's side.

'And I thought we had all the worst fog back in London,' he said. 'Makes you wonder how anyone ever managed to find the way to the North Pole.'

'Or to Russia,' said Tommy Tilson.

'I see the Old Man's on the bridge again.'

'Ah – that means we must be getting close to the convoy. Another ship, that's all I want to see; another bloody ship. It's like everything round here has died.'

'Aye – a floating graveyard, that's what it is.'

James walked breezily past the men at the ship's rail.

'Cheer up, my bonny boys – get ready to splice a few mainbraces and all that.'

'Get stuffed.'

'What, *again*?' he said with mock incredulity.

Later, the daymen were making fast one of the crates for Murmansk, which had worked itself loose, when the solitary figure of Alastair was seen staring out to sea. He was as still as a statue, hardly seeming to blink or even breathe, so intent was his vigil.

'There he is – at it again, the poor bleeder.'

Suddenly the Stornowegian jerked into life and shouted, pointing up at the overcast sky. Seconds afterwards there was another shout from one of the bridge lookouts and the *Lady Emma*'s alarm-bells clanged twice.

143

'Aircraft alert!'

Men scrambled to action-stations and Lieutenant Hadley studied the sky through his binoculars. A faint droning was heard from an unseen plane passing high above, and as they listened it gradually became louder. The plaintive sound booming through the overcast was unmistakable.

'It's Wandering Willie again.'

'What's he on now – the milk run?'

The black dragon-fly shape was briefly seen in the greyness of sky, but was quickly swallowed up again and lost. They heard it circle around overhead then drone away in another direction, the ominous pulsating sound fading away to the merest murmur, until it was finally gone. They remained at action-stations, but as time wore on without further incident the tension eased and men relaxed and laughed and joked, and mugs of tea were called for. The trawler had not altered speed, although the wary McBride had changed her course slightly to take advantage of the outer fringes of the fog, offering as it did a friendly and sensible cover.

Sub-Lieutenant Grant nodded to Price at the setting-dial of the four-inch. 'All right – you can return to aft lookout. Tilson, take over.'

Price left the gun platform, got down the steps to the deck and walked off past the messdeck hatch, then the Wardroom hatch, and was rounding the base of the bridge structure when he was seized by a fit of coughing, caused by a combination of tickling fog and dry throat. Even as he spluttered it seemed to him that the beat of the *Emma*'s engines had grown stronger, producing an odd kind of noise, but the strangeness of it did not connect in his mind until he was threading his way past the depth-charge throwers, making for the boat-deck. Then, with a sudden overpowering sense of there being something wrong, he turned to look for'ard, being aware of scattered shouts from several parts of the ship as he did so. The extra noise he had heard was coming not from the ship but from a new black shape now hurtling low out of the sky, a black bat growing rapidly larger, and as he gazed at it in horror his legs did not know what to do – to carry him further on his way to the boat-deck or turn and take him running back in haste to rejoin the four-inch crew. But the distance he had now covered decided him. He could hardly have reached the gun in time, nor was there any immediate purpose in his reaching the boat-deck. He stood stock-still, hoping in a foolish kind of way that if he froze and did not move an inch he would escape bullet or bomb.

He saw the bombs distinctly as they were released by the Junkers 88, three small black objects looking like tiny Indian clubs, twisting and waggling as they grew larger and more menacing. All the sights and sounds that followed merged into one hasty, blurred pattern. The vibration of the *Emma* as her engine revs increased in an effort to take the ship hard to starboard into the fog and out of the path of the bombs . . . the great clouds of black smoke pouring from her funnel . . . the thunderous roars of the four-inch as it got away three rounds in quick time, only for them to explode astern of the Junkers . . . the boom of the plane as it soared overhead with its five-man crew clearly visible . . . the first two bombs, hitting the water in line off the port bow, sending up huge waterspouts and causing the ship to shudder; then the disappearance for a fraction of a second of the third bomb, until the explosion as it slammed down on the trawler's battered bow.

There was a gigantic flash, followed by a deafening eruption, and clouds of swirling smoke obliterated the whole of the bow. The ship lurched alarmingly. Both Hotchkiss gunners sent streams of fire after the German plane and the point-five opened up until the air was filled with flying lead. But the Junkers veered sharply and regained height until it was out of danger and zoomed off into the grey sky.

'Campbell! Stretcher party for'ard!' Lieutenant Hadley shouted the command as he swiftly descended the bridge ladder.

'Aye, aye, sir! Price, help me, mon!'

Price ran over to the Buffer, who sent Eddie Nash and Jack Barrow for the two stretchers. Campbell gave him the medical box to carry. 'D'ye know the first-aid?'

Price nodded, although he had never yet had to bandage a finger. Through the smoke pouring up from the bow he could see the torn and twisted gun platform and the barrel of the four-inch pointing drunkenly upwards. No one was moving – could anyone have survived that direct hit? No, for God's sake, they couldn't all be gone, the survivors must be sheltering under cover . . .

'Look out!'

At the urgent cry he turned seaward and saw a second Junkers homing in on the ship, seeming to scatter aside the fog in its flight. It was approaching squarely amidships and screeched towards them at frightening speed. Nash and Barrow, on emerg-

10   145

ing with the stretchers, threw them down and dived to the deck.

'Get down!'

Campbell ducked to his knees but Price lingered, fascinated, to see the plane release its bombs, his limbs totally unable to move. Then he felt his legs roughly snatched from under him and he fell heavily, banging his head on the deck.

'Do you want to be bleedin' killed?' yelled Eddie Nash savagely.

As the plane roared overhead it swerved to port to escape the blasting point-five and soared away into the distance. Again the first two bombs fell into the sea, the second one so close to the ship's side that its waterspout rose in the air and smacked down on the four of them with an icy weight of water that left them gasping and groping as the ship was lifted bodily and sent reeling to starboard. She had hardly begun to right herself when the third bomb struck on the starboard side, blasting the bridge and filling the air with a mad whirl of flying wood and metal.

Drenched and dazed, his face bleeding from several cuts, Price scrambled to his feet and looked up at the bridge. The gunner on one Hotchkiss had vanished, while at the other gun, Sam the fisherman lay in a crumpled heap. The bridge itself was severely damaged and there was no sign of the Skipper. He looked for'ard after the stretcher party, which had gone on without him. The smoke over the bows was clearing and he could now see bodies on the deck, but none was moving. He was aware of Barrow pausing in his rescue work to shake an angry fist to the sky, his mouth opening and shutting but no sound seeming to come from it.

'Peter!'

Price looked back at the faint cry to see Brewster emerge staggering from the wheelhouse, pointing aft at a third Junkers coming in quickly. Convinced now how he could help, Price ran urgently for the bridge wing and one of the Hotchkiss guns, but he was beaten to it. The flying figure of Harrigan, no limp discernible now, reached the portside gun, roughly rolled aside the body of Sam, seized the Hotchkiss and spurted bullets at the diving plane, his snarling curses unheard in the din but leaving nothing to the imagination. At the same time the other Hotchkiss kicked into action, operated grimly by Sub-Lieutenant Sibley, hatless and hair askew. The gun spluttered and stopped as he struggled with the ammunition belt, then it began firing again in steady bursts.

Brewster was running aft. Price started after him, but the

point-five was still fully manned and he changed his mind and turned back, thinking he would be more useful in the wheelhouse, but before he could enter it the third Junkers was upon them. A dark shadow passed over the funnel and another violent explosion, which shot him sprawling to the deck, blew an enormous hole in the boat-deck and the engineroom casing, hurling the point-five gun platform with its three gunners, and the whaleboat, part of the funnel and a mass of deck fittings into the sea. All that remained after the explosion was another gaping hole with thick black smoke pouring from it. Smoke, intermingled with fog, now encircled the whole ship as she settled in the water, having lost all way, flames blazing from the three main areas where she had been struck. She was helpless and finished, but still, astonishingly, afloat.

Stemming the blood from his face with his sleeve Price saw Lieutenant Hadley lying stretched out full-length on deck, one of his legs twisted awkwardly, and ran across to the No. 1, kneeling down to help him.

'No,' gasped Hadley, his face creased with pain, blood on his lips, 'leave me. On the bridge, Price – the switch – to flood the magazine. Do you know the switch? Hurry, man, hurry!'

He knew the switch. The Buffer had described it to him when they had talked about the store of explosives carried by the trawler. As an emergency measure there was a large water tank above the magazine and the pressing of the special switch on the bridge would let tons of water down to render all those shells and depth-charges safe from fire. He ran as ordered, and in his climb heard himself giving little gasps and moans in his urgency. Half-way up the bridge ladder he looked down and could see moving figures on deck as well as sprawling bodies. He saw Ginger Meeson. The big man was slumped in a sitting position, supporting himself with one strong arm and pawing his chest with a massive hand, looking in bewilderment at the blood which came away on it. As Price reached the top of the ladder and made for the bridge door which hung shattered, half off its hinges, he heard a weak shout from the deck of 'Abandon ship!' Inside the bridge-house he came unexpectedly upon McBride, lying on his back beside the smashed chart table, eyes wide open and blood oozing wet on his neck. Price stopped instinctively, half expecting a sharp command to be barked at him from the craggy face. But the eyes were unseeing. McBride was dead.

He raced across the shambles of the bridge, to the flooding

147

switch, only to find to his dismay that it was no longer there. The entire panel had been torn away, leaving only a tangled mass of wires. Sick at heart he looked out at the Hotchkiss guns. The port gun was no longer there, neither was Harrigan, while at the starboard Hotchkiss, Sibley was slouched back with arms dangling and his face unrecognisable, covered in blood, a tragically mute and blighted figure.

The smell of burning was fierce in the air, and as he hurried back down the ladder the realisation that the magazine could go up at any moment came home to him with full force. On reaching the deck and scrambling over the debris to Hadley he found the No. 1 lying still. He crouched down to him, but the officer, with blood trickling from the corners of his mouth, was dead.

'The rafts! Get the rafts!'

He turned at the cry to see men trying to free the rafts and floats, and was about to run over to help when he was halted by an appalling sight. A grotesque figure came staggering and reeling towards him, the face so swollen and bloated as to be scarcely human. It was Barney the stoker. Shreds of clothing hung from him and the flesh beneath was stripped off to show bare bones. The mouth opened and closed but no sound came. He had been descending the ladder to the engineroom when the bomb hit and had taken the full impact of scalding steam bursting out of the boiler. He collapsed at Price's feet and lay there quivering. As Price stared helplessly at the pitiful, dying man he heard a yell and a splash as someone jumped overboard and knew on the instant that he must do the same – the ship was in blazing ruins and the magazine would blow up any second; there was no time to lose. He ran to the rail where the water was coming over the deck, took a deep breath and fell over into the sea head first.

The douching embrace of the freezing water almost knocked him unconscious. Down, down he went until in his panic he feared his lifejacket would never arrest his descent and he struck out with flailing arms and legs to try to stop himself falling like a stone to the very bottom of the yawning ocean depths. Somehow he managed to cling on to sensibility and work his arms properly to give himself lift, but his lungs were bursting and it seemed that he would never make the surface. When he did, there was time only to take another great breath before something dark and blunt rammed him hard in the forehead, then rose up to obscure the grey daylight and banged down on his head. He began to fight again, to hit and claw and scratch his way past the obstacle. In his terrible frenzy he started to go down once more, but again used his arms to bring himself back to the surface. This time he bobbed clear of the piece of timber which had blocked his way, and quickly grabbed it and clung on to it for support.

The ship was behind him now in the fog, furiously ablaze, and he started to paddle himself away, fast, faster, with no other thought than that of putting as great a distance as he could between himself and the doomed vessel. He began to tire and to feel the cold keenly, but was determined to keep going as long as his numbed, sluggish limbs would allow. He was still weakly pushing himself along when the sea suddenly heaved and shivered, shaking him loose from the supporting timber, and the tremendous blast as the *Lady Emma* disintegrated into a thousand pieces rumbled far and wide and rolled upwards to the heavens. On looking back as the sea subsided he could see nothing but fog where the trawler had once been. Starkly conscious of his helplessness he searched around anxiously for the lost piece of timber and, on sighting it, kicked towards it until he had clutched it and felt once more its reassuring support.

What to do now? On the one side there was nothing but a vast expanse of sea, and on the other the foggy emptiness over the spot where the ship had vanished. But, strangely, he had no hesitation in deciding his next move. The *Lady Emma* afloat, had represented safety and comradeship, and though she had now gone he must go back to her, or at least to where she had been. To find what? He did not know or try to understand, only began striking out in the water with his free arm.

It took an age. He was becoming heavier in the water and there was the feeling that a great suction lurked around his legs, eager to pull him down. He was now intensely cold, his spine like an icy tube. He willed himself to find body warmth, to ward off the encompassing, deadening chill which threatened to creep up and strike through to his heart. He knew that if it did, he would be finished; even now it would have been so easy just to give in . . .

He neared some floating debris, then lost sight of it in the fog. Panic struck again and he became aware of fog all round him and overhead, a dark, stifling curtain cutting him off from the sky and the whole world. He was going to sink, to drown. He began to paddle furiously and tried to work his legs. He was so intent on regaining some feeling in his body that when a shape loomed up alarmingly in his path he agitated the water and struck away from it with the wildest of fears, but the terror passed when it dawned on his fuddled brain what it was – one of the *Lady Emma*'s Carley floats. Paddling madly back towards it he caught hold of a becket and clung on with all his fast-ebbing strength, an effort that caused him to let go of his supporting timber, which quickly shot out of reach. He had no choice now. Calling on every ounce of strength and will he grasped the rope lashings round the raft and battled to drag himself up and over the hard cork side. It seemed an impossible task, but he refused to be beaten, and fell over at last into the float's 'deck' of open planking, where he lay utterly exhausted. It was tempting to remain there but he knew he must get up and sit on the side; in a swell the sea came up through the planking, the big float being merely an enlarged version of the old cork lifebelt. He righted himself, shivering, making sure to hold on to the loose ropes lashed in a series of 'diamonds' round the float's sides. Using one hand at a time he tried to slop and squeeze water from his clothes and to work his tired limbs to keep the circulation going. He shook and shivered himself into a semblance of warmth, examining the float as he did so. It was undamaged, but both of its paddles were missing. He started to call out, for the sake of hearing his own voice if nothing else.

'Hello! ... Hello! ... Hello!'

There was no answering shout from the depths of the fog. He slapped and rubbed his legs and wriggled his ankles. He must at all costs keep the use of his legs. The cuts on his face were smarting, his head throbbed, his stomach was seized with a creasing pain as it recovered sensitivity against the cold.

'Ahoy, raft!'

It was a weak, despairing cry from close at hand. A struggling swimmer appeared and, splashing forward, tried to grasp the trailing ropes, but failed. Price lay down full length on the float, his head and an arm over the side to give assistance, and when the hand reached out again he grabbed it and clung tenaciously to the wrist.

'Thanks, Pricey,' gasped Jack Barrow hoarsely. In the same second the light went out of his eyes and he said no more, his head flopping down into the water. Price fought to drag him up the side, and when he could not, attempted to force Barrow's hand round a rope, but all the use had gone from it and as the raft bucked and reared in the water the dead hand slipped from

150

his grasp and Barrow's lifeless body wallowed and floated away in the swell.

Price dragged himself up again and sat with head bowed. There was nothing more he could do; the strong, tattooed body had broken and died, vanishing into the fog. Forcing himself to keep active in spite of heavy remorse, Price first secured his feet then tightly folded and re-folded his arms, trying to press some warmth into his sodden and sorely aching body. He must work at it, and work, and work . . .

For an hour or more he floated aimlessly in the fog before seeing a dark object faintly in the distance. He strained his eyes – it looked like a boat! He tried to paddle the Carley float in its direction with his hands, but his clumsy efforts made no impression and the boat was steadily receding. It *was* a boat, the *Emma*'s whaler, clearly damaged, with its upper sides misshapen, but well afloat.

'Ahoy, whaleboat!' he cried excitedly, but his voice now was only a croak. 'Ahoy there!'

He had to take the risk – the boat was possibly his last chance of survival. Nerving himself against another freezing immersion he lowered himself into the icy sea and kicked out for the whaler. Although making vigorous kicking motions with his thighs he could feel nothing of the legs below them, and just hoped fervently that the lower legs were doing their part. This they must have done, for eventually he reached the whaler, hung on to it with one hand and peered over the side. There were two men in it, both stretched out, one half sitting.

'Hello, Peter Price,' said James.

Price smiled through his cracked lips, and in his surprise and delight nearly lost his hold of the boat, but after a heart-stopping moment he grasped the side of the whaler with both hands and painfully hauled himself up and slithered and fell over into it.

'Excuse me if I don't get up, dear boy,' said James hollowly. He lay with one arm doubled up beneath him, the other holding on to the remains of a smashed seat.

'Are you hurt?' Price gasped.

'Never mind me, see to the kid.'

Brewster lay in the forepart of the boat, his legs dangling in water which the two of them had been unable to bale out. Price bent down to him.

'Eric?'

Brewster did not reply. His eyes, showing only fleeting recog-

151

nition, stared up at the fog, and he did not move.

'Blankets,' said James with an effort. 'The drinking water's gone, locker's blown out, no food, but get the blankets.'

Price found the blankets. Only three remained and he took one across to Brewster, lifted the boy's feet out of the water in the bottom of the boat and tucked the blanket round him. Still he did not move, and he was breathing painfully. Price eased himself over to James and put a blanket over him. As he did so James shrank into himself and groaned as the edges were pushed in round his body.

'Steady – I'm not much use.'

'Your arm . . . '

'Leave it.'

Price pulled the remaining blanket round himself and sat down. He felt sick and his head was bursting.

'I . . . can't talk much – good thing, eh?' said James with the ghost of a smile.

'What happened to you?'

'Hit – in the back. Jumped – found the boat – pulled the kid in . . . ' James started to cough again, wincing at each spasm, but when Price made to move towards him he shook his head. 'Stay put – but keep working your legs. Think yourself warm, Pricey . . . *think* . . . ' his voice trailed away as he breathed hard, in obvious pain.

There was no oar in the damaged boat and no rowlocks to fit one. The rudder was smashed and useless. The boat was simply a floating shell, the miracle being that its hull had remained intact when blown from the trawler. With the continual swaying Price felt his stomach beginning to retch although he knew there was nothing inside him to be sick. For minutes he struggled to keep a hold on himself and finally pulled out of a gathering black inertia to glance across at Brewster. The boy was so still. He edged towards him and saw that his eyes were now closed and his fresh features, which seemed to have grown unaccountably smaller, were at peace. The suspicion came to him and he squatted down beside the body, only to confirm his fears. The boy had breathed his last.

'Take his blanket,' said James flatly.

When he did not move, James said again, 'Take it. He doesn't need it now.'

But Price did not take the blanket. Instead, he drew the upper edge of it over the silent face. James sighed, but said nothing more as Price settled himself back in the middle of the boat, his groggy legs only just able to answer the call made on them. The restless fog kept wisping, clearing, then rolling back to enshroud them, never remaining still. They seemed to be moving, but it was only the motion of the sea. He felt he could not hold off his sickly drowsiness much longer, that he must slip away . . . but eventually James spoke again, a small voice, far away, and he roused himself and edged along the boat towards him. James stared up, almost as if seeing right through him; then he blinked, indicating that he wanted Price to bend down close to hear him.

'I'll tell you . . . something . . . Peter Price,' he whispered hoarsely. 'Dying . . . doesn't hurt . . . '

His head fell to one side and he had gone.

Price turned away, burying his head in the crook of his arm. From that moment on reality took flight. He was so racked with bitter sorrow, so sick, so alone, his emotions had reached snapping point. And he was so desperately drowsy. He made a last try to rouse himself, but his eyes remained half closed and the eyelids wanted to clamp shut, his head to loll, as a great fatigue came over him in a wave, issuing up from his numbed legs and robbing the rest of his body of all resistance. He fought again to keep his eyes open, to move his arms, his wrists, his fingers, but all the strength and will to do so drained and ebbed away until his weary eyes closed and he sank back in a sleep-bound stupor, oblivious to his freezing surroundings.

He was transported to a sunlit green field.

'Come on, Peter, *over*arm,' his father was saying, standing smilingly ready at the wicket with his bat. The young boy bowled his best, only to see the ball stroked half across the field. 'That's better, son, again now . . . ' The picture changed suddenly, jerkily, as in one of those books where the pictures moved into life as the pages were flicked between finger and thumb. He was lolling on a rug before a blazing fire and could hear the chink of cups in the background as his mother prepared tea. His mother's face became superimposed on the picture, showing clearly in every detail, and then his father's face merged with it, and both were smiling. The picture flickered again and blurred to emptiness.

Then another change of image. 'I'll be paying in next month as usual,' the nervously confidential man at the bank counter was saying. 'Tell the manager all I need is the fourteen pounds to tide me over . . . ' The pictures stopped and there was only a dull, bottomless void. He floated in timeless space, his outward physical senses all gone, and yet the whole of him curiously warm. He seemed to be dwindling in mass to something very small and negligible, and falling, falling . . .

It could have been after seconds, minutes or hours when his passage to oblivion was halted abruptly. He was conscious of a voice which seemed to be coming from the end of a long, long tunnel, and as his salt-caked, frozen-rimmed eyes fluttered half open he heard an answering voice. In hollow, croaked tones it sounded words that were only just recognisable.

'Who . . . are . . . you?'

He was dimly aware that the questioning voice was his own. Then the first voice came again, shattering the tunnel and booming through his aching head.

'*Marigold.*'

With painful effort he screwed up his eyes to see the face pushed anxiously close to his. He saw first a nose with little black hairs protruding from the nostrils, then a darkish jaw with a mole on it, searching green eyes under black eyebrows, and a grey balaclava encircling the rest of the head, like a soldier from Norman times as sketched in a school textbook.

'The corvette *Marigold* – is there anyone else?'

Price stared up at the face of his rescuer. He tried to speak again but his dry, swollen mouth was incapable of forming the words. Gently the big sailor took him up in his arms, like a baby. Then the dam broke.

'All right, lad, all right . . . ' The strong arms gave him a reassuring squeeze, but he now had no control over any part of his body. He sobbed and sobbed, the tears streaming down his face, and the more he shivered and shook and tried to hold back, the more the tears gushed forth.

'There, there . . . don't worry, lad, let it go, let it go . . . '

He sobbed until the face of his rescuer suddenly blanked out and he knew no more.

15

A bird was singing throatily outside the open window of the Commander's office. Out of the blue sky, a probing shaft of spring sunlight spilled across the floor of the room, lending colour and warmth to its bare, prefabricated walls. The Commander was speaking, but Price heard only half of what he said, his thoughts had wandered too far away.

'We have your full report – and I commend you on its clarity – but we shall want you back for the adjourned Court of Enquiry. However, I shall see to it personally that this does not interrupt your training course at King Alfred.'

Yes, it was all in the report which lay on the Commander's desk at his fingertips. Everything, from start to finish. Everything, that is, except his days here in the Naval hospital in the South of England. The fever and the nightmares with him strapped to his bed in a rabid delirium, the bed heaving and tossing as it took on horrific life alternately as the reeling, broken, burning trawler and the bucking whaleboat. The familiar figures bobbing up and down and accosting him in his dreams, passing by in an endless parade, laughing and dying and then unaccountably reappearing alive again and joking. 'Never mind, tea at the "Albert" when we get in . . . '

'What's that?' said the Commander.

'Nothing sir, I was just thinking . . . '

'Are you all right, Price?'

'Yes, sir.'

'You're sure?'

The Commander looked him over shrewdly, then walked across to the window and gazed out on the English morning. He himself was enduring a restless spell of shore-time, being a casualty from action in the North Atlantic. Although he was not yet thirty he had acquired in a very short time the experience of a man twice his age, yet even so he found it difficult to guess at the true emotions of a lone survivor. The right words, if there were any, did not come easy at such a time.

'It's a beautiful morning,' he said, and walked back to his desk, drumming the fingers of his right hand lightly on it as he seated himself. His other, injured arm dropped to rest on his lap like a bird's broken wing. It itched and ached in its hospital trussings.

'I see you wish to remain, if possible, with the Royal Naval Patrol Service?'

'Yes, sir.'

'I think I understand.'

Did he? Maybe he did.

'I hope you do well on your course. I think you will. Good luck.'

'Thank you, sir.'

Later he saw the M.O.

'Legs all right now?'

Yes. At first it had been too painful even for them to be touched by the bedsheet, the nurses had had to put up a kind of wire cage over his tortured limbs to allow him to sleep. But now, thankfully, the tenderness had almost gone.

'You're a very lucky young man!'

Yes, he was, but he did not know why. All the time he had been asking himself, why? Why me?

Afterwards, by his bedside, he packed his kit. It was all newly drawn from the clothing store, for he had lost everything. Into the canvas bag they went. Spare uniform, two Naval collars, two seaman's jerseys, three pairs of cotton pants, three cotton vests, three towels, PT vest and shorts, one pair of plimsolls. The packing took a long time; a Naval kitbag was not the lightest of luggage. Two pairs of woollen gloves, one pair of leather gloves, one heavy woollen jersey, one sou-wester, one scarf, one balaclava . . .

'Patrol Service? That's the trawlers, isn't it?' an interested stores Petty Officer had said. 'Pretty rough, I'm told.'

Yes, he had said, it was, and hurried on. By now he had become used to being regarded as something of an oddity among the rank and file of personnel who came from the 'proper Navy'.

He left hospital the next day. The train was crowded, full of tired men, and made many stops and starts on its long journey with bursts of snorting, spouting steam from the harassed loco-motive. On its arrival at the big inter-change station he took his gear to the left luggage office, where it could stay until he returned to resume his broken journey, then caught a second, smaller local train. An even slower journey. On leaving this train he felt somewhat naked, being without luggage, while other Servicemen among the passengers toiled with their kitbags and suitcases. As he left the platform, his green travel warrant duly inspected, a busy WVS woman smiled across from her laden refreshment trolley.

'A cup of tea, son?' she offered encouragingly.

'No – thanks,' he said, and felt mean at refusing, but to stop now, even for a few minutes, might make him falter in his intention. He made straight for the station entrance, past an array of strident posters.

'CARELESS TALK COSTS LIVES . . . BRITAIN SHALL NOT BURN . . . LET US GO FORWARD TOGETHER . . . JOIN THE WRENS AND FREE A MAN FOR THE FLEET . . . '

It was raining and he looked out on to drab, wet and shiny streets. He knew exactly where to go, as he had made inquiries beforehand; his destination lay only three streets away. He stepped out into the rain, walking quickly so that he would not have second thoughts and be tempted to turn back.

He was nervously apprehensive and did not know what he would say – he could be doing totally the wrong thing. But he had to go on.

He had to see Enid, and try his best to explain.

PQ17 – CONVOY TO HELL

by Paul Lund and Harry Ludlam

In June, 1942, Convoy PQ17, consisting of thirty-five merchant ships, set out for Russia with an escort of cruisers and destroyers. They had a reasonable chance of success until the order came to 'Scatter!'

What followed represents one of the most terrible and tragic blunders of the Second World War.

Authors Ludlam and Lund give a first hand account of the horror and despair that faced the men left to the mercy of a cruel enemy. From thousands of sources and recollections they have built up an unforgettable picture of what it was like to be in PQ17 – and survive...

NEW ENGLISH LIBRARY

TRAWLERS GO TO WAR
by Paul Lund
and Harry Ludlam

The story of Harry Tate's Navy. Officially it was called the
Royal Naval Patrol Service – a rough and ready fleet of
hastily-armed trawlers and drifters. Manned almost
entirely by Royal Naval Reserve fishermen the little ships
did heroic service as mine-sweepers, convoy escorts
and – audaciously – hunters of U-boats.

Through 'E-boat Alley' and up the Channel, to America,
Africa and India, into the bone-freezing waters of the
Murmansk convoys, the old trawlers with their outdated
guns made their nick-name of the 'Harry Tates' a password
for courage of the highest order.

NEW ENGLISH LIBRARY

NEL BESTSELLERS

T035 794	HOW GREEN WAS MY VALLEY	*Richard Llewellyn*	95p
T039 560	I BOUGHT A MOUNTAIN	*Thomas Firbank*	90p
T033 988	IN THE TEETH OF THE EVIDENCE	*Dorothy L. Sayers*	90p
T040 755	THE KING MUST DIE	*Mary Renault*	85p
T038 149	THE CARPETBAGGERS	*Harold Robbins*	£1.50
T040 917	TO SIR WITH LOVE	*E. R. Braithwaite*	75p
T041 719	HOW TO LIVE WITH A NEUROTIC DOG	*Stephen Baker*	75p
T040 925	THE PRIZE	*Irving Wallace*	£1.60
T034 755	THE CITADEL	*A. J. Cronin*	£1.10
T042 189	STRANGER IN A STRANGE LAND	*Robert Heinlein*	£1.25
T037 673	BABY & CHILD CARE	*Dr Benjamin Spock*	£1.50
T037 053	79 PARK AVENUE	*Harold Robbins*	£1.25
T035 697	DUNE	*Frank Herbert*	£1.25
T035 832	THE MOON IS A HARSH MISTRESS	*Robert Heinlein*	£1.00
T040 933	THE SEVEN MINUTES	*Irving Wallace*	£1.50
T038 130	THE INHERITORS	*Harold Robbins*	£1.25
T035 689	RICH MAN, POOR MAN	*Irwin Shaw*	£1.50
T037 134	EDGE 27: DEATH DRIVE	*George G. Gilman*	75p
T037 541	DEVIL'S GUARD	*Robert Elford*	£1.25
T042 774	THE RATS	*James Herbert*	80p
T042 340	CARRIE	*Stephen King*	80p
T042 782	THE FOG	*James Herbert*	90p
T033 740	THE MIXED BLESSING	*Helen Van Slyke*	£1.25
T037 061	BLOOD AND MONEY	*Thomas Thompson*	£1.50

NEL P.O. BOX 11, FALMOUTH TR10 9EN, CORNWALL

Postage charge:
U.K. Customers. Please allow 22p for the first book plus 10p per copy for each additional book ordered to a maximum charge of 92p to cover the cost of postage and packing.

B.F.P.O. & Eire. Please allow 22p for the first book plus 10p per copy for the next 6 books, thereafter 4p per book.

Overseas Customers. Please allow 30p for the first book plus 10p per copy for each additional book.

Please send cheque or postal order (no currency).

Name ....

Address ....

....

Title ....

While every effort is made to keep prices steady, it is sometimes necessary to increase prices at short notice. New English Library reserve the right to show on covers and charge new retail prices which may differ from those advertised in the text or elsewhere.